The Thrall

by Njord Kane

Published on: June 1, 2016 by Spangenhelm Publishing

Interior Design and Cover by: Njord Kane

Library of Congress Control Number: 2016938507

ISBN-13: 978-1943066-100

ISBN-10: 1943066108

1. Fiction 2. Fantasy 3. Historical Fiction

First Edition.

10 9 8 7 6 5 4 3 2 1

Table of Contents

No kitten was harmed in the production of this book.

Chapter 1 – The Longhouse

In a glaciated valley where rocky green slopes descended into the crisp blue waters of a long narrow Fjord, there stood the tall mossy thatched roof of a longhouse.

There was nothing particularly special about this long pitched roof from any of the other long pitched roofs scattered about on the sloped hills leading into the fjord. Except this particular long pitched roof belonged to the household of Bjord Thorsson, the local blacksmith.

Bjord's longhouse was easy to pick out because of the black smoke that often bellowed out from the fires of his forge burning inside. One didn't suffer the cold of winter inside the house of a blacksmith.

Inside lived the ever busy household of the blacksmith. Most of their daily toils were conducted around the central fire pit in the very heart of their home.

The aroma of fresh rye bread filled the air inside the house. Gwenda, Bjord's wife, was busy making bread. She always made extra knowing that it would be gobbled up with the fresh cheese she had to go with their meal.

They already goggled up nearly half of it with the leftovers of yesterday's bread early this morning.

Her mother Helga sat near the fire with her distaff and was diligently spinning wool. She hummed an old lullaby in some old and forgotten language. Nobody in the house understood the words except Grandmother.

Nobody really knew how old Grandmother Helga really was. Gwenda had once confessed to her husband when they first married that she wasn't really sure if Helga was her mother or grandmother.

Helga maintained many of her old habits and always wore a scarf over her grayed hair, which she put in a partially braided bun.

The smell of fresh bread wasn't the only thing permeating the air of the longhouse. Near the fire hung a haunch of mutton, rubbed with dried sweet grasses and honey, that slowly smoked.

Directly over the fire hung a black kettle that had been fabricated years ago by her husband's father's father. A tribute to the durability of the skilled blacksmiths that had been passed on their trade generation after generation.

The pot was slowly being filled with chopped root vegetables by the blacksmith's daughter Thelsa. This would later become the stew for the evening meal. Seasoning and chopped slices from the smoking mutton will be added to it later.

Thelsa was a young girl who was just a few Yules past puberty and already she looked just like her mother when she was a young woman herself.

At one end of the house was the byre where the family's livestock was kept. There were three cows and six sheep in the byre, not to mention one temperamental goat, which the family appropriately named, "Grumpy."

Grumpy didn't like being with the rest of the livestock. He felt he was much too important to be considered with the cows and the sheep. He never stayed in his pen. Most mornings, members of the household would awaken to see Grumpy standing over them and staring them in the face, chewing on whatever mischief he got his chompers into this time. Whenever anyone got up to put him back into his pen, he'd protest with a loud bleat and have to be dragged back into his pen as he resisted the whole way.

On the other end of the longhouse was where Bjord worked his trade. It was the blacksmithing area. There was a large forge and an anvil stone that set deep into the ground.

The anvil stone was much too large to have been brought into the house when it was built. The blacksmith's house was built over the massive anvil stone to accompany the smith's needs.

It was upon this anvil stone that Bjord was busy pounding away upon a piece of red hot iron.

Bjord was a large middle aged man with a thick bushy beard. Strains of gray wove their way through the dark curls of his beard. Lines of experience ran across his face to match that helped reveal his age.

His long bushy beard was most likely a compensation for his balding head. Something Bjord would never admit. However, balding or not, he still grew out what little of it was left and tied it back into pony tail by a leather cord.

Bjord preferred to wear heavy leather boots and brown leather pants due to his trade. It only takes stepping on a hot piece of iron slag once to make a blacksmith prefer wearing leather boots. He also wore a loose undyed sleeveless tunics, which was always dirty and stained black due to the dirtiness of his profession of working iron. He also wore a leather apron that protected him from the flying sparks when hot iron was struck.

Bjord was striking hot iron now. He was making an ax head for chopping wood. Each swing of his hammer made the tell tale sound of metal clinging that rang through the walls and echoed out into the stillness of the surrounding area.

He worked with precision as he banged away, shaping the heated chunk of iron gradually into the shape of an ax head. His arms were as strong as the iron he worked from many years of pounding metal into its new shapes.

Along the walls hung various tools that the craftsman had made that he had available for trade. Besides tools, there was also a variety of spear heads, shield bosses, and battle axes as well. The blacksmith specialized in both the tools of war and labor.

The axes he made were for a variety of uses and styles. Axes had existed as a part of his people's culture since before any elder can remember. It was customary for just about anyone within their culture to wear one in their belts. Even thralls that were bound in servitude to their masters, wore an ax.

The axes they wore on their belts weren't

particularly large. The handles were no longer than a man's forearm and the ax heads were no larger than a man's outstretched hand.

The large battle axes were usually only carried when going to battle. They had larger bearded ax heads and long handles that made them nearly as tall as a man. A few of them hung peacefully on wooden pegs along the wall.

Also hanging along the wall were painted round wooden shields. They were made from planks of linden wood so they were less likely to split in combat. All shields had iron bosses with handles in the center. Some of them were even reinforced with leather and had a band of iron around them to help reinforce their strength.

Hanging near the shields were a few iron helms and a couple of partially completed chainmail shirts as well. The chainmail was usually worked in the wintertime, when the cold and snow kept everyone inside their longhouses. This was when time allowed for the more tedious demands it took to make such items.

Chain mail armor had hundreds of rings that needed to be riveted and linked together with unbroken rings in a precise pattern. A finished mail coat would bring the blacksmith quite a bit of silver, making it well worth his effort.

Assisting the blacksmith in his work was his son Sven, whom was also his only apprentice. Sven, although tall for his age, was skinny in contrast to his father's muscular bulk. His bushy dirty blond hair was cropped at shoulder length and was as wild as his temperament.

It was always a tangled mess when his mother would try to tame it with her comb. Sven wasn't too particular about how his hair appeared. This annoyed his mother to no ends.

Sven didn't care much for the laborious life associated with blacksmithing. This was to his father's annoyance. He often daydreamed of a life of adventure and longed to be part of the heroic adventures of going viking.

He never dressed in the woolen trousers or tunics that everyone else wore. Instead, he insisted on wearing linen clothes and soft leather leggings that laced up almost to his knees. He dressed for comfort, not work.

Sven was working the forge's bellows and watching his father's hammer blows on the hot iron in order to learn the trade himself. The forge's fire was kept hot by the bellows pumped on the side which forced air into the burning coals, making them glow hotter.

Bjord was focused on his work and kept a steady rhythm. He shaped the red hot iron until it needed to be put back in the fire to be reheated. The hammer's chime only stopped when he thrust the iron back into the forge's hot coals and barked out, "bellows!"

Sven responded with a startled jump from the sudden roar of Bjord's voice and grabbed the handle of the bellows. He pumped the bellows in a steady and deliberate tempo. The rush of air immediately made the fire glow hotter, sending tiny sparks and smoldering embers into the air mixing with the smoke.

Sven hated working the bellows, it was a job for a thrall, not an apprentice. Especially if the apprentice is the blacksmith's son. But once again, working the bellows was his task. It was always his task and he hated it.

Bjord set his hammer down on the anvil and with his iron tongs grabbed the piece of iron he was working and turned it in the hot coals. The piece of iron was already starting to glow red again from the forge's heat.

He wiped a line of sweat off his brow as he watched the piece of metal glow even more reddish orange from the heat. Experience taught him just when the metal was hot enough to work by the color alone.

He looked at his son Sven, whom was staring out the door and daydreaming again. It was obvious how disinterested he was in what he was doing.

"What's the matter boy, am I working you too hard?" remarked Bjord, not really expecting an answer.

"No, I just think I'm ready to work the iron and not always work the bellows like a thrall."

"You don't always work the bellows. Besides, I have the thrall busy with other things, unless you want to trade him places." Bjord snorted. "If you think you're ready to shape the iron, then tell me if this piece of iron is ready yet. Is it hot enough? You should be able to tell by now from its color alone."

"Yes, it's ready." answered Sven without much confidence.

"No it is not." Bjord angrily scorned. "You still have much to learn, boy! If you'd spend more time paying attention when I try to teach you this trade instead of daydreaming and wishing you were somewhere else, you might actually learn how to do this and become useful."

Bjord wasn't happy about his son's lack of enthusiasm to learn the family's trade. It wasn't something you learned right away nor learned passively. It took great attention of detail to work metal.

Looking at his son, who was once again looking out the doorway and daydreaming, Bjord decided to send him off to do something else.

"You're irritating me right now, boy. I have the thrall out sheering sheep. Go out there and help him gather the wool or something."

Sven looked at him with a visibly hurt expression on his face. He couldn't believe he was being told to go help a thrall.

"Make sure the wool is washed so it can be hung to dry and be put on a distaff as soon as possible. Go now, don't just stand there looking at me." Bjord barked as he reached over and took over pumping the forge's bellow.

Sven hesitated for a moment, but he knew not to make a protest. "Go now boy!" Bjord barked one last time as he grabbed the tongs and shifted the iron heating in the coals.

Sven did as he was told and moped his way out the door towards where he heard the sheep bleating. He muttered a few whines of self pity under his breathe as he walked away, but made sure his father didn't hear him.

Chapter 2 - The Thrall

Amongst the household dwelt a thrall named Rowan. He'd been in the blacksmith's household since he was a small lad. He was sold to the blacksmith by a trader whom had found him in the burnt rubble of his family's longhouse in another land called Jutland.

Rowan was too small to remember who the invaders were that attacked and destroyed his village, but he knew his village were a tribe of people called the Hard-Jutes.

The trader that found him came the morning after the invaders had left to scavenge through the village's ruins. While rummaging, he discovered Rowan hiding under a table in the ruins of his charred home.

The trader gathered small boy up, along with what household items of value remained and sailed off.

Rowan was put aboard a knarr boat that had a huge red and white striped sail, marking it as a merchant's trading vessel.

They sailed across the cold waters of the sea towards the mountainous lands of the north. Their boat fought across a violent and angry sea. The knarr crashed over the savage waves as the wind howled terrifyingly beyond the darkness. Rowan held on for dear life as he watched with wide eyes, the men aboard the ship laughing loudly at the angry sea, mocking it.

The trader tied Rowan to the mast and then reassured him, "don't worry boy, the gods aren't coming for you today!"

When the sea calmed and the morning mist lifted, Rowan could see that they were sailing along steep bluffs until they finally broke open to reveal pristine fjords.

Along one of these fjords, the trade ship ported at a village that was inhabited by other folk that belonged to a different tribe similar to his own folk that were now gone. Rowan would soon learn, this was the Hard-Anger tribe.

When he was disembarked, Rowan was hoping to be adopted by one of the villagers, but was sold immediately as a thrall to the blacksmith.

The blacksmith had bought him for less than the price of a calf and immediately put him to work chopping wood for the house's fire and stacking coal for the blacksmith's fiery forge.

Mind you, although he assisted the blacksmith, he was not a blacksmith's apprentice and was not trained in the trade. He was but a lowly thrall dressed in a worn tunic and woven pants. The first thing the blacksmith had put on him was a ring around his neck revealing this status.

His dirty blonde hair was also cropped short, common to that of a bond servant. His duties varied from tending to the household's livestock to gathering wood to whatever he was told to do by anyone in the blacksmith's house. He'd been in the Blacksmith's household for ten winters now.

Today, Rowan was out herding the newly shorn sheep when Sven arrived.

"I'm here to take over herding the sheep, you're to go and wash the wool." Sven said in a resentful tone while looking at the ground avoiding eye contact.

Rowan knew because of Sven's tone and manner and the fact that he was here to take over herding the sheep instead of helping his father that he'd probably been scorned again for not paying attention.

Rowan nodded at him and headed towards the side of the longhouse where he'd left the sacks of wool. Sven coming to take over herding the sheep was fine by him, he needed to gather up the fleece skirts so they could be washed anyways.

Grandmother Helga had shown Rowan how to wash the wool in a particular manner in which she insisted on. It required lots of rinsing and took Rowan longer to get it done to her specifications, but it always paid off. She'd reward him with a candied biscuit she made from honey comb and dried blueberries.

Rowan was fond of Grandmother Helga. Even though he was a thrall, she never treated him as such.

Helga also insisted on being the one who carded the wool. She always used her special combs with strange symbols carved on them. She'd quietly sing to the wool as she carded it.

Rowan spent the remainder of the daylight washing the wool and laying it out to dry. Hopefully, he'd get his reward for doing a good job on the wool tomorrow.

Chapter 3 - Late in the Night

It was late in the night when Rowan woke up startled. He felt like he was drowning in his sleep. He dreamt that he was in the water of the fjord and someone was standing on his chest holding him down underwater.

Although he'd awakened, it still felt like something heavy pressing down on his chest. Groggily, he opened eyes and was startled to what he saw. There was a rather large house cat sitting on his chest.

It just sat there looking down at him with its yellow eyes that seemed to glow in the darkness and look directly into his soul. It was the biggest cat he'd ever seen. It wasn't a mountain lion or anything like that. It was just a simple orange house cat, but it was biggest house cat that he'd ever seen.

Rowan wasn't sure if he was still half asleep and dreaming or what, but the cat seemed to be getting heavier and heavier as it sat there on his chest. It wasn't even moving, it was just sat on his chest staring down at him. It had the weight of a large man.

The cat's unusual weight had Rowan pinned down and he couldn't move. It was making it harder and harder for him to breath.

Rowan made a desperate attempt to get the cat off him, as it was definitely getting heavier and heavier. It was now making it impossible for him to breath, crushing his chest under its impossible weight. He tried to roll to his side and knock the cat off him, but he couldn't move. He was pinned down under its weight as it seemed to grow even larger.

He was suffocating under its weight and couldn't yell out. He needed to wake someone up and get help. He had to get the cat off his chest before it killed him.

In another desperate attempt, he threw up his legs and tried to force the cat off him. The cat leaned his head down closer to him and hissed the most horrible and eerie hiss he'd ever heard loudly in his face. At that moment, the cat leapt off from his chest as Rowan choked and gasped for air.

The cat's screech alerted the entire household out of their slumbers. After leaping off Rowan it ran towards the byne and leapt towards the livestock, all of which were all wide eyed and now in panic.

The ghastly screech the cat made as it ran caused the sheep to charge out of their pen and break through the door in a frenzied attempt to get away for the cat.

The cows ran to the opposite side of the house, where the goat was already perched from its usual rebellious nightly escape.

The panic stricken sheep ran screaming outside into the darkness and out of sight with the ghoulish cat in hot pursuit howling demoniacally behind them.

Everyone in the longhouse quickly rose wide eyed and in a panicked frenzy. Nobody knew what was going on. It was the most frightening and unnerving sound ever made by the animals, sounds never heard before. It was terrifying.

Bjord sprang from his bed and quickly ran over to grab a torch by the wall. He lit it from the central fire pit and then used it to look around the longhouse. Seeing no threat, but terrified animals, he rushed outside to investigate. He could still hear the sheep screaming as they continued to run in the darkness outside.

Everyone else, including Rowan, rushed outside

behind him. Sven grabbed a torch and lit it from the hearth fire, he also grabbed an ax to arm himself. The fear in his eyes was obvious. He wasn't about to step outside unarmed.

The sheep were gone. They could still be heard off in the distance madly running up the hill in the darkness. The unnatural howls of the cat chasing behind them could also be heard. It was obviously trying to run them to their deaths.

"What just happened?!" demanded Bjord as he turned around towards everyone with an angry look on his face.

Rowan, half afraid to answer and a bit unsure himself of what had just happened answered, "a feral cat. I think."

"A cat?" inquired Bjord. "Are you kidding me?"

Rowan nodded and said, "I was sleeping and woke up to a cat sitting on my chest."

Bjord cocked his head to the side and looked at Rowan oddly.

Rowan nodded and added, "even stranger was that it got heavier and heavier as it sat on me. I wasn't sure if I was dreaming or not until it started to take away my breath."

"It tried to take away your breath?" Bjord asked

unbelieving.

"Yes, from the weight. It kept getting heavier and heavier. It was as if it was trying to crush me. When I tried to get it off me, it got even bigger and heavier until I couldn't move or breathe at all."

Bjord was starting to get angry at this point, listening to this nonsense.

Rowan, still trying to convince him added, "I managed to roll to my side a little and that was when it hissed, jumped off me and then chased after the sheep."

Everyone looked at Rowan bewildered.

This is when Grandmother Helga spoke up and said, "that was no cat. That was a draug." She had been standing behind everyone, looking from the doorway.

"A draug? What's a draug if I dare ask." asked Bjord in an almost mocking tone.

"Yes a draug, a dead walker." she replied back with a scornful tone. "It's a person that has risen from the dead and now walks the Earth cursed by its own obsessions or hatred."

"Oh yes, I remember my grandfather telling stories about dead walkers. But he also spoke of many other unseen beings in the forests and mountains from the myths of old, such as trolls and elves too. Nobody's ever seen such a thing and I don't mean any disrespect, but Grandfather also used to run outside naked flapping his arms squeaking like a bird." Bjord said with a laugh, referring to when his grandfather began to become a bit 'touched' in the head the last years before he died.

Helga just looked at him with contempt for his mocking. She threw her arms up as she turned around and went back inside.

"I suspect that it will run the sheep to their deaths. That's what the ancient legends say they do. It's fortunate that the cows ran in the opposite direction and didn't run with the sheep, otherwise they'd be lost too," she added as she disappeared inside.

Bjord angrily responded, "I'm not going to lose my sheep to a damned feral cat. Dead walkers are nothing but superstition."

He turned towards the boys and said, "Rowan! Fetch my ax and grab some torches. We're going to get those sheep back."

Rowan immediately jumped into action upon Bjord's command. He ran inside and grabbed Bjord's battle ax that hung near the blacksmith's favorite place to sit. He briefly looked at Bjord's shield that hung next to it and pondered whether or not to grab it as well, but decided against it. He scrambled to grab an armful of unlit torches and ran back outside with his bundle, handing the ax to Bjord.

Bjord turned towards his son Sven, "Boy! Grab some rope in case we need to tether any of the sheep to bring them back."

Sven ran inside to gather some rope as Rowan busied himself binding the extra torches together with some twine. He then improvised a strap and slung the bundle of torches across his back.

Sven and Rowan shared a look when he came back outside with the rope and tossed it on the ground in front of Rowan. Rowan knew how lazy Sven could be and without changing beat, picked up the rope and slung the rope over his shoulder.

Meanwhile, Bjord was standing at the edge of the treeline where the sheep had ran, staring into the darkness while contemplating whether or not to try to find them in the dark or not.

Sven and Rowan quickly joined him and quietly stood behind him waiting for instruction.

After a few moments, Bjord still holding the torch in the air while looking into the darkness said, "we're not going to find them in the dark. We will have wait until the morning when we have sunlight."

He turned around and looked at Sven, then at Rowan and then back at Sven again before saying, "let's get some sleep and go after them in the morning."

Chapter 4 - The Mound

The morning came fast, with little sleep for the blacksmith's still shaken household. The events just hours ago had left everyone sleeping with one eye opened and their ears perked for even the slightest sound. Nobody was granted a restful sleep.

Rowan couldn't find it within himself to sleep lying on his back for fear of the thing coming back and trying to seat itself on his chest again.

Perhaps this time it would be successful and end him before he'd be able to wake up in time. This time he slept, or rather attempted to sleep on his side to prevent anything from resting on his chest.

When the light shined through the doorway and announced daybreak had come, Rowan was relieved. He was tired, but glad to have made it through the rest of the night.

He knew he'd better not dawdle in his daily

tasks, so he got up and went to the byre area to milk the cows. Being mindful not to disturb anyone, he fetched the milking bucket and noticed that the goat was on the other end of the house standing on the anvil looking back at him.

Obliviously, Grumpy didn't get any sleep as well and had kept a vigilance throughout the rest of the night perched up on the anvil stone.

Rowan smiled thinking, "don't worry goat, I didn't get any sleep either."

He slowly positioned himself around the cow, being mindful that it may still be a bit skittish from last night. After a moment of reassuring the cow and feeling that it was calm enough, he reached down to began milking her. Just before he got the first drop, Rowan noticed something in the milking bucket.

It was something wrapped in a piece of cloth. Rowan reached down in the bucket and picked it up. It was a piece of Helga's scarf. He unwrapped it and found one of her honey biscuits. Rowan smiled.

He quickly wrapped it back up and stuffed it in his shirt.

The milking had to be done first thing in the morning. Gwenda wanted to make as much cheese as possible before the cows started to slow their milk giving at the end of the season. The milk would have to set out and curd. He began steadily milking the cow.

A sudden voice came from behind Rowan, startling him and made him slightly jump. The cow he was milking was also spooked and mooed in protest while taking a step sideways.

It was Bjord. Rowan didn't hear him get up while he was busying himself with the milking.

"Forget the milking today and let Thelsa finish doing it."

Rowan looked up at Bjord and nodded. He then stood up and hung the milking bucket on a hook that was on a support beam so the cows wouldn't kick it over.

"Thelsa! Get up!" Bjord barked, loud enough to stir everyone in the house out of their peaceful slumber. "Finish the milking!"

Thelsa, still dazed in the drink of sleep, rubbed the tiredness from her eyes and started to get out of bed.

"That's the thrall's job..."

"Do what I tell you lazy girl!" scorned Bjord cutting her off before she could finish protesting.

He turned back towards Rowan and said, "gather several fathoms of rope, enough to tether each of the sheep if we need to."

As he gave Rowan these instructions, he walked by Sven's bed and kicked him on the bottom of his feet. "Get up boy, it's time to fetch those sheep."

"Make sure you grab your bow," he further instructed his son as he gathered supplies himself, stuffing them into a leather shoulder strap bag.

Gwenda got up and headed towards the cooking fire. "Do you want me to cook you anything before you go?"

"No, I'll just grab some dried meat to take with us. I don't think we'll be gone very long."

Bjord walked over to where Gwenda was standing and grabbed some dried meat that was hanging next to her. He cut off several chunks and stuffed them into his shoulder pack.

"Those sheep couldn't have ran off very far," he said with one final word before embracing his wife and then turning to head out the door.

"Come on boys, I want to get this over with. We have lots to do when we get back. There's really no time to be messing around looking for skittish sheep."

The three of them, Bjord, Sven and Rowan, exited the longhouse and set out in the direction the sheep had ran off last night. They followed the livestock's trail left behind as it led across the field and into the woods. Heading directly up the hillside.

Rowan didn't like the idea of going into the forest up the hillside. He had a bad feeling about it. The sheep were always too skittish to even get close to the wood line. It was just something they'd never do for fear of predators ambushing them. They always wandered in the other direction and steered way clear of the woods when they grazed. It was a bit odd that they'd intentionally run into the woods. Albeit, they were being chased by something horrifying.

Rowan shook these thoughts off. Such worrying thoughts were meaningless. There wasn't anything that happened last night that made any sense. So why should the sheep running in the woods make any sense.

After awhile, the trail began to lead into the thicker trees and brush of the forest that went up the mountainside. This area was seldom, if at all, ever ventured into by anyone from the village. Superstitious or not, nobody wanted to chance venturing too far into the wilderness and never being heard from again.

Ahead of them, Bjord noticed something whitish in color in the bushes. He stopped in his tracks trying to see what it was. Sven, not really paying any attention, kept walking. Without looking away from whatever was in the bushes ahead, Bjord reached his arm out and caught Sven by the shoulder as he walked past him, stopping him.

"Look," he said to Sven, pointing at the bushes ahead of them. "There's something in that bush."

Sven looked around for a moment, but didn't see anything. Then he noticed it and gasped.

"Go see what it is."

With a gulp, Sven looked back at his father horrified. But before he could answer, Bjord stepped forward to look himself. "Never mind boy."

Sven cautiously stood behind Bjord to get a better look at what it was.

It was one of the sheep.

"That's one of them, " Sven confirmed as he looked over his father's shoulder. "It's been freshly shorn and its wearing one of our collars."

All the livestock that belonged to the blacksmith's house wore a leather collar that had a single iron ring hanging from it inscribed with the word, "Bjord" to mark his ownership of them.

Even Rowan's neck collar was inscribed similarly with the word, 'Bjord.' Except instead of leather,

Rowan's collar was made from iron.

"You could tell it ran itself to death, its eyes are still wide open from fear." Bjord pointed out while still looking at it.

Rowan said nothing regarding it and just stood there looking around. This place made him feel uneasy. Something about these woods just wasn't right and he knew it. He knew not how, but he just knew they should not be here. The sheep weren't worth whatever awaited them.

Sven looked at Bjord for a moment and then said, "I'm hungry, can we stop and eat?"

Bjord turned around and looked at him for a moment. He was just about to say something, but then dropped his shoulders and softened up.

"Yes, we should rest a moment and grab a bite to eat. There is no sense continuing on with an empty stomach."

Bjord removed his shoulder bag and sat on the ground with his back to a tree. Sven and Rowan sat down next to him as he reached into his bag and pulled out a thick slice of meat. It was a slice from a haunch of smoked boar.

He broke the chunk of meat in two and handed the smaller half to Sven, keeping the larger for himself. Rowan wasn't given anything to eat and just sat there awkwardly waiting for them to finish.

After about twenty minutes or so, Bjord satisfied he'd eaten and rested enough, put the remainder of his chunk of meat in his bag and stood up. He wiped his hands on his pants and dusted off.

Rowan taking the hint, stood up as well and adjusted the rope he was carrying over his shoulder.

Bjord looked down at Sven. He was still eating and ignoring everyone.

"Come on boy, you can eat that as we go. We haven't got all day."

Without waiting for him to get up, Bjord turned and began walking through the woods, following the trail the sheep had made. Rowan followed behind him, taking a final look at the dead sheep on the ground.

Sven got up and followed, taking a few more bites off his chunk of meat before deciding he had enough and tossed it into the bushes. Rowan heard him throw it and heard it hit the ground as his stomach slightly grumbled. He didn't give Sven the satisfaction of looking, he was quite used to this kind of treatment. Besides, tucked under his shirt, wrapped in a piece of cloth was one of Helga's honey biscuits. He'll enjoy that himself later.

As a thrall, he wasn't mistreated in general or even abused. He knew he was fortunate to be owned by the blacksmith as he'd seen how other thralls were treated by other owners. Many of them abused and quite often beaten. Rowan had never been beaten and even though he had no intention of running away, he still had to wear the neck ring. There were just times like this when his status, for some unknown reason, was made clear.

Bjord motioned forward and said, "come on, we've got to find the others."

They continued to follow the trail left behind by the running sheep pack. Sven and Rowan followed behind Bjord as he tracked their way up the mountain. The route was gradually starting to incline steeper as they went further.

The men were starting to sweat and Bjord stopped and sat down on a rock to rest. The younger two sat down on the ground near him. It was then that Rowan noticed that something just wasn't right around them.

The forest was just simply too quiet.

The usual sounds of wildlife and birds were missing. There was an unsettling stillness in the forest. The only thing that could be heard were the occasional sounds of leaves rustling when the wind blew, but that was all. It was too quiet.

"Do you hear that?" Rowan asked nobody in particular.

Bjord listened for a minute and said, "what? I don't hear anything."

Sven, who had also listened, nodded in agreement. He didn't hear anything either.

"Exactly. There's no sound, not even the birds are chirping." Rowan pointed out.

Sven began to look openly worried, but Bjord shrugged, stood up and said, "come on, we've got to find those sheep."

They continued up following the trail until they came upon another dead sheep lying on the ground halfway in a bush. It was like the first one, you could tell it ran itself to death in total fear. Sven shuddered at the sight of it.

"Rowan, pull that sheep out of the bushes." Bjord said. "I want to be able to find it on our way back. I am sure we can salvage some of the meat from it."

Rowan did as he was told and pulled the sheep out of the bush it had fallen into when it died. Sven stood back and watched, offering no assistance. Not that Rowan expected any help, he was used to Sven idly watching him. It just amused him how Sven

38

seemed to be afraid of it.

After Rowan had the sheep pulled away from the bush Bjord turned and continued walking up the hillside. There was still a visible track and he followed the remaining trail up the hill.

"Keep moving, there's still four sheep that may still be alive. That is, if the wolves don't find them before we do."

As they proceeded further up the hillside, ever determined, the trees and brush began to get even thicker. Even though it was only mid day, the density of the foliage was starting to make it darker and darker around them.

Pushing their way through the brush, they suddenly were overwhelmed by the most horrendous smell of rotten decay.

It seemed to be thick in the air and clung on everything like a thick invisible fog. It permeated the air as if it had been there for quite awhile.

Sven gagged and said, "what's that smell? It's awful!"

"Something dead nearby. Keep going, it'll pass." said Bjord as he used his arm to cover his mouth and nose.

Rowan had never smelled anything like it before.

He'd once came across a rotting boar carcass in the forest when he was gathering wood. The boar was discolored, bloated, and putrid. It was definitely dead and definitely had been there for a while. It laid in a patch of sunlight that beamed in through a clearing of the trees. It was so putrid, not even the flies wanted it.

The smell in the air now was similar, but way worse. It made Rowan's stomach churn in a most unpleasant way. He tried using his sleeve to cover the smell. It didn't even help.

By the looks on Sven and Bjord's faces, they were just as disgusted and feeling just as green as Rowan was.

The men stopped in their tracks. They were all trying to cover their noses and mouths as best as they could. Bjord looked at them and said, "well,.. [he abruptly stopped to gag] we've indeed found something unpleasant lurking about here. Something's definitely dead near here. I don't think it's any of the sheep. They haven't been dead long enough to rot and smell like that. Plus the other sheep we found didn't smell."

Sven and Rowan both nodded in agreement not wanting to speak and uncover their mouths.

"Whatever it is, it's been dead for awhile. I don't

know what would make such a stench, but I don't think I want to find out." Bjord added.

The notion made both Sven and Rowan turn pale as their hearts fearfully sank. They've all heard the stories about the things that supposedly lived in the forest and in the mountains. Places said to be forbidden to men where both unseen folk and beings from the legends were said to inhabit.

In the brush, they could clearly see where the remaining sheep had ran. They ran right through, breaking limbs and everything else in their way, as if they were desperate to escape whatever was chasing them.

The entire way had been this way. It didn't take any real tracking skills to follow the panicking sheep's trail. In this spot, the trail ran right through some dense bushes.

Bjord scratched the back of his head and knelt down to examine the torn bushes. "They must have been cornered and ran right through it." He plucked a piece of wool from a branch and stood back up.

"Yes, I do believe that is what happened. Here's a piece of wool from one of them. They tore through those bushes and made their own path."

Sven and Rowan just looked at each other, not sure what to think about the whole ordeal.

After a moment of kneeling back down and trying to look through the hole in the bushes, Bjord stood up and motioned to Rowan while pointing at the hole, "crawl though there and see if you can tell where they went."

Rowan silently gulped and nodded. He wasn't sure what lie beyond those bushes and whether or not he wanted to meet it face to face while crawling on his knees through some bushes.

He removed the rope he was carrying over his shoulder and set it down on the ground. He got down on his hands and knees and carefully began crawling into the hole in the bushes. He could see light on the other side. It looked like it was quite a few paces from where the sheep had gone in and then busted out on the other side.

Rowan crawled through hole. It was only as high as he was on his knees and barely as wide as his own body. He continued to crawl through to the other side.

When he came out through the other side Rowan got quite the startle as he almost fell.

Abruptly on the other side of the thick bushes and brush that the sheep had ran though was a steep cliff. It was a very steep cliff that dropped for a long way.

42

Rowan backed up carefully, as not to fall off the side. "There's a cliff at the other end of these bushes!" he shouted.

Bjord hollered back, "what? What do you see?"

'There's a steep cliff that goes down the mountainside," repeated Rowan.

Bjord drew his brows together and wrinkled his forehead, giving Sven a puzzled look.

"Do you see any of the sheep?"

Rowan edged closer to the side and looked over. All he could see was a abrupt decline that fell several ways down into the rocks below. He gasped and safely scooted himself back again. He turned and yelled back, "I don't see them. It falls straight down into rocks. There is no sign of them down there."

Bjord looked down, sighing in his breath and mumbled something about 'thralls.' He looked back up at Sven and said, "go in there and look. Tell me if you can see where the sheep went."

Sven did not want to go in there. Regardless of his daydreaming, he wasn't exactly 'hero' material. But before he could make any kind of protest, Bjord frowned at him and motioned towards the hole torn in the bush.

"Go now boy!"

Sven nodded and removed his bow and leather weaved quiver. He set them down on top of where Rowan had set the rope. He reluctantly knelt down to crawl through the hole and paused a second to look through. He then looked back at his quiver real quick to make sure he had set it down so that none of the arrows would fall out. This was when he noticed that he'd grabbed the wrong quiver.

The quiver he'd grabbed in his haste contained fishing arrows with the arrow heads made from bone. They had small barbs in them and shattered when they hit against anything. They were not the sharp iron tipped arrows for hunting.

He grabbed the bow and arrows in case they came across some wolves or something and needed to defend themselves.

He hoped his father didn't notice his bumble. He seriously doubted that he'd need his bow, but he didn't want to catch hell for grabbing the wrong quiver of arrows.

Bjord grew openly annoyed at Sven's hesitation and kicked him on the rump with the side of his foot. "Get in there boy, stop being a damned coward."

Sven crawled through the passage to where Rowan was knelt down on the other end. He crawled through, tearing a hole in his trouser knee, and knelt next to him.

Sven carefully looked over the edge to see what was there. Rowan grabbed Sven on the shoulder and steadied him as he got near the edge. "Be careful." he said.

He just shot Rowan a dirty look and said, "don't worry thrall, I've got this."

Sven hesitantly looked further over the side and carefully scanned the area below in disbelief. Seeing the rocks below from the sudden long drop, he backed up and looked at Rowan with a look of baffled disbelief on his face.

Rowan nodded in agreement and looked over the side again himself.

Sven backed up from the ledge slightly and called back. "It's true. There's a sudden drop over a cliff at the end of the passage. It's a long drop and there are rocks below. Nothing could survive that kind of a fall."

"Do you see any sign of the sheep?" Bjord called back.

"I don't see any sign of the sheep. It's like they just disappeared. I can't say for sure, but I don't see their bodies anywhere down there."

Puzzled, Bjord angrily cursed under his breath.

"Go ahead and come back through. Make sure you look one last time to make sure there's no sign of them. They had to go somewhere. Things don't just disappear in thin air."

"We're coming back out," Sven called back. He didn't need to be told twice to get out of there. He didn't want to crawl through that hole in the first place. And he absolutely did not like being next to that cliff with its sudden drop to a guaranteed death.

Sven began crawling out through the hole with Rowan following closely behind.

When Sven got through, he quickly stood up and quickly began brushing the dirt from his hands and knees before gathering up his bow and quiver.

Rowan crawled out and picked the rope up from the ground, slinging it back over his shoulder.

The air was still thick with a putrid smell from something dead and rotten. Sven covered his nose and mouth with the inside of his arm, trying not to gag. When they had crawled through the hole, the air on the other side was much clearer and didn't reek. It was only when they crawled back that it hit them again.

"What is that smell?" protested Sven to nobody in particular.

Bjord answered, "I don't know, but it can't be from the sheep. Even if they'd been dead for a long time, they wouldn't leave behind a stench such as that. This smell is from something that has been rotting for a very long time. It is unnatural."

After a brief moment Bjord decided to continue looking for the sheep. There was no real proof that they ran over the cliff. Although something could have carried them off below, such as wolves or other wildlife. But they also could have seen the cliff and turned around.

He wasn't going to be satisfied unless he'd given the area a proper look.

"Let's go further up the hill and see what we can find out. Maybe the sheep ran up there. The brush is very thick, but we can still get through this way." He indicted which direction by pointing to a less dense area and started walking towards it.

Bjord led the way as they made their way through the thicket up the hill. He used his ax to chop some of tree limbs out of the way to allow for their passage.

The smell of decay was getting even more intense. Sven stopped once when his stomach couldn't handle it anymore and retched out his earlier meal.

Rowan secretly got some satisfaction from observing this. Sven hadn't the common compassion to share his meat and tossed the remainder in the woods. Having an empty stomach now paid off for Rowan. Even though he wasn't sure for how much longer.

Alas they finally got through and came out of the thick brush to a clearing on the other side. On the clearing there was very little brush. It opened up to a clearing that was mostly rocky. Nothing seemed to really grow there and in the middle of it all was a mound of piled river stones and dirt.

The mound also appeared to have been freshly made.

The putrid smell in the air was now worse than ever at the clearing where the mound was. It smelled as if there were rotting corpses all over the place. There was nothing but this barren mound of stone and soil.

Gasping from the stench in the air, Sven asked, "what is this place?"

"I don't know," replied Bjord "it appears to be a burial mound."

"A burial mound?" said Sven in near disbelief. "Are you sure?"

48

"Yes, I know a burial mound when I see one." said Bjord. "But what I don't get is why it's way up here hidden in the forest on the mountain and why the dirt is so fresh. It looks like it was just made."

Rowan just stood behind them, covering his nose and mouth, trying to not get sick from the stench that lingered in the air.

Bjord walked toward the burial mound to inspect it more closely. The other two moved slightly closer behind him, but still kept their distance.

"I don't understand why it smells so bad,' said Bjord as he looked at the mound closely with his eyes visibly starting to water from the offensive smell in the air.

"What do you mean?" asked Sven.

"Well for one, whatever is buried here shouldn't be smelling like this because it's buried," he pointed out "and there's nothing exposed here to make the smell."

Bjord bent down on one knee to get an even closer look at the earth mound, brushing some of the soil on the mound to the side.

"Yes, this soil seems fresh on this." He observed. "Even stranger is whoever made this used river stones."

"So what? Lots of people do that." said Sven.

"Yeah, but not way up here on the mountain side. They had to carry those stones up from a river. Why didn't they just use the rock that was already here?"

It was then when they noticed a heavy mist beginning to form around them. It was originating from the mound itself.

Sven and Rowan exchanged a worried look.

"This is very odd," Sven said. "Mists don't just form out of nowhere and they don't form that fast. Something isn't right about this."

Bjord stood up and looked around. Just as he was about to say something, they all noticed a dark figure standing in front of them on top of the burial mound. It just sort of 'appeared' in the mist.

The smell of death in the air was stronger than it had ever been before.

"What is that?" asked Sven as he gagged from the stench in the air.

"Who's there!" Bjord demanded of the large figure standing in front of him in the mist.

Bjord lifted his battle ax up in front of him. He gripped the handle tightly with both hands and and briefly looked at Sven and said, "get an arrow ready, boy," before looking back at the figure.

The mist was starting to fade away and they were able to get a better look at the figure.

It was twice as tall as a man and bloated twice as wide. Its rotting flesh was pink and purplish blue. with dead white eyes glaring through swollen eyelids.

The smell of decay that came from it was so strong it sickened everyone to a point of actually wanting to drop to their knees and start gagging. It made them want to wretch, but fear from the very sight of this thing prevented any action but gazing at it in horror.

It was the draug, the dead walker that Grandmother Helga warned of.

It stood there for a moment looking at them menacingly before it let out a piercing scream and leapt forward at Bjord.

It pounced on top of Bjord before he could react. Still in shock, even though he had his ax at the ready, it was useless in his hands. Bjord fell to the ground on his back with the creature on top of him.

You could see Bjord's face turning red as he struggled under the weight of the beast. It had him pinned down. Its knee was on his arm and prevented him from raising his ax.

Bjord was pinned and helpless. He was completely unable to defend himself. That was when the ghastly thing brought its huge fist down upon him and smashed him in the chest. The powerful hit made Bjord gasp painfully for air before spitting out some blood.

Both Sven and Rowan stood frozen for a moment with their mouths agape looking on in shock before they were able to react.

Sven, seeing that it was killing his father, grabbed his bow and retrieved one of the bone tipped fishing arrows. He nocked the arrow, drew back and released it into the side of the dead walker.

The beast was so large, it was nearly impossible to miss as the arrow struck its target and pierced deeply into the creature's rotting flesh.

The arrow strike didn't even phase it and it struck Bjord again with its massive fist while letting out a horrifying roar.

Sven released another arrow, piercing it again which also seemed to have no affect on the beast. It was as if the thing didn't even notice the arrows Sven was firing into it.

Rowan was now able to move from the initial shock. He took his small ax from his belt, gripped it loosely on the end of the handle and then hurdled it at the beast.

He was hoping to sink the ax blade deep into the monster's skull. The ax hurdled through the air and swished pass the creature's head, missing completely and fell in the thick brush behind it. Lost forever.

Rowan just stared in disbelief at the brush where the ax fell. He didn't know what made him think he could actually hit the creature with it. He'd never thrown an ax before. He'd seen one of the men from the village throw one into a tree truck and was impressed by it. He didn't considered such a skill would actually take practice.

Now he was disarmed because of his foolish act.

Sven paid no attention to what Rowan was doing and sunk another arrow into the beast. Regardless of yet another arrow finding its mark and sinking deeply, the beast continued to ignore the arrows as if they weren't even there.

The dead walker was in a fury. It continued to strike at Bjord, whom was no longer moving and no longer appeared to even be alive anymore.

Rowan now disarmed and knowing he had to do something, mustered the courage to get closer and try to fetch the large battle ax that Bjord had dropped when the creature leapt upon him.

After taking a quick second to gather his courage, Rowan ran towards the ax. He slid across the ground feet first trying to keep low and out of the beast's reach. As he was sliding past the creature on the dirt and gravel, he managed to grab the battle ax off the ground.

Rowan got back up to his feet and picked up the ax with both hands. It was a large, heavy and solid ax. Gripping it tightly, he raised the ax above his head and then brought it down upon the beast with all his might.

He hit it and sunk the ax's blade deeply into the creature's back.

In contrast to the arrows it ignored that were embedded in its flesh, the creature felt the ax penetrate. It violently roared in pain and turned around, swatting Rowan with the back of its fist.

The blow knocked Rowan back several feet, causing him to tumble hard to the ground.

Rowan had never been hit that hard in his life. He was now dazed from the blow and had the wind knocked out of him. He struggled to get up to his knees as he looked up at the creature. It was violently turning about trying to grab the ax that was stuck in its back.

Sven continued firing his remaining arrows into

the dead walker with no affect. The beast was completely unconcerned with the arrows and appeared to ignore them. But the ax embedded into its back definitely had its attention as it continued to struggle trying to reach the ax and pull it out.

When the creature turned its back towards Rowan, he could see that the ax was actually burning the creature's decaying flesh.

He could see around the wound where the ax was stuck in its back and he could see that its flesh was glowing red like a hot iron. There also was some smoke coming from around the wound where the ax was embedded.

It looked like the ax head was actually burning its flesh.

Sven fired his last arrow into it and then threw his bow down on the ground. He grabbed the ax that hung on his belt and armed himself with it.

The beast was still reeling in pain and trying to free the ax from its back.

Sven looked at Rowan and could see that he wasn't armed and was still struggling to get up to his feet after being knocked back so hard from the beast.

Sven knew what he had to do. He mustered all the courage he could and charged at the creature. He swung his ax upon it and sliced it on the arm. The creature released an ear piecing roar and turned to face Sven as he swung his ax at it again. This time only nicking it on the forearm.

This only angered the creature even more. In a fury it reached over and grabbed Sven by the head with its massive hands. Before Sven could react and swing his ax again, it flung him in the air and into the brush near the side of the clearing near the cliff.

Sven hit the ground hard and dropped his ax. He nearly tumbled over the cliff when he hit the ground. The wind was now knocked out of him and he struggled to get up, but was unable.

He must have broken a few bones when he hit the ground. Pain radiated all through his body placing him on the edge of falling unconscious. He tried to call out for help, but was only able to spit out blood as he slumped on the ground.

The dead walker clinched its fists and angrily roared at Sven as he struggled on the ground. Rowan was able to get to his feet and looked around for a weapon. A rock, a big stick, anything he could use as a weapon.

The dead walker was infuriated. It stomped over to where Sven was laying on the ground, broken and in terrible pain. It briefly looked down at him and then grabbed Sven by the chest and leg. It picked him up and lifted him up above its head while letting out a ferocious roar before it threw Sven's broken body over the side of the cliff.

Sven couldn't even scream.

Rowan was unarmed and there was nothing he could do. He could see that the ax he embedded into the back of the creature was still burning it. After it hurled Sven over the cliff, the creature continued struggling trying to reach the ax and pull it out from its back.

Rowan knew he wouldn't be able to take the creature out. He managed to wound it, but that was pure luck and he no longer had a weapon anyways.

He took one last look at Bjord's lifeless broken body on the ground and then turned towards the clearing in the brush they originally came through and ran for his life.

He charged through the partially cut branches as if they weren't even there. Pushing through the brush in a desperate fury to escape the deadly wrath of the dead walker.

As he passing through the thickest part of the brush, he heard the beast roar behind him. It noticed him fleeing. Just as Rowan passed through and reached the other side where they tracked the sheep, he heard the beast howl again and then start charging through the brush after him.

Rowan looked around in every direction trying to decide what to do. If he ran down the path they came up, the beast would surely catch up to him and run him down.

He looked through the hole in the bushes where the sheep had ran over the cliff and decided to crawl through it in an attempt to hide. He quickly crawled through, scrapping himself by the broken branches as reached the other side. By time he got to the other side where the cliff was, he heard the dead walker growling on the other side where he had just been seconds ago.

It would have easily overcome him if he'd ran down the trail.

The dead walker didn't continued down the pass chasing after him as Rowan had hoped it would. It knew he'd gone through the bush to hide. Rowan knew he would have to do something quick. But what? He was cornered at the edge of a steep cliff with no where to go.

Thinking quickly, he realized he still had the rope slung over his shoulders. He removed the rope and took hold of one end. He looked for something to tie the end of the rope on. If he could secure the end of the rope, maybe he lower himself down the side of the cliff to escape the creature.

Rowan searched for something sturdy to tie the rope to and decided on the base of a bush that appeared to be deeply rooted.

The creature was getting closer, but was struggling to get through the hole.

Rowan's hands were shaking as he tied the knot and secured it to the base of the bush stump. He then quickly tossed the other end down the side of the cliff.

He could hear the dead walker starting to tear its way through the bushes towards him. It was coming after him and would reach him any second. There was no time to waste. It was do or die.

Having no other choice, Rowan began climbing down the rope over the side of the cliff.

As he lowered himself down he heard the dead walker roaring. He looked up and seen it looking down at him, towering over the edge of the cliff with a broken bush hanging off it where it had tore its way through the brush.

Rowan began climbing down the rope even quicker in his desperate attempt to escape. He didn't even know if the rope was long enough to reach the bottom or not, but he had nowhere else to go.

The creature grunted as it reached down and grabbed the rope. Rowan felt the rope being pulled up and seen the creature was hauling him up.

He began sliding down the rope in a desperate attempt gain distance between him and the creature. His hands burned from the friction of the rope as he loosened his grip to slide down it.

Looking down, Rowan noticed a ledge on the side of the cliff and tightened his grip on the rope, stopping his slid. The friction burn cause Rowan to wince in pain bu the managed to stop himself.

He began trying swing himself towards the side of the cliff and was almost able to reach a root that was sticking out of the side of the cliff above the ledge. He felt the rope being tugged and being pulled up ferociously.

The creature was going to pull him up if he didn't do something now.

Burning his hands even more, he slid down the rope even further only to discovered that he was now at the end of the rope and couldn't go down any further.

The creature kept pulling the rope up.

Rowan would have to make a desperate lunge for

the root that hanging from the side of that cliff. He swung hard one last time before he felt the rope being pulled up again. Rowan let go of the rope as he swung towards the cliff side and tried to grab the protruding tree root.

Despite his best effort, he fell short of the tree root and crashed hard into the face of the cliff wall.

Rowan then fell from the side and down onto the lower cliff ledge. Luckily he didn't fall to his death, but he was still too high up and fell hard on the ledge's rocky surface. When he landed on the ledge, he dropped so hard that he managed to hit his head on a rock.

The world went black as Rowan was knocked unconscious.

Chapter 5 - The Long Way Back

Rowan woke up to rain drops hitting him in the face. Groggy and hazy, he slowly opened his eyes and looked around. Seeing the ledge he was on, he quickly remembered where he was and what had happened.

His body ached in nearly every place.

He noticed that he was laying on the edge of the cliff's small ledge, so he carefully sat up and shifted himself back safely away from the edge. His head pounded with a throbbing pain at the back of his head and neck.

He looked around hardly able to believe he was still alive. Recapping the events of everything that had taken place, he realized what had happened when he fell and why his head hurt.

It looked like it was early morning. He'd been knocked unconscious when he landed and must have slept the rest of the day and through the night.

It was now raining lightly. He wasn't soaking wet, so it must have just started. Rowan looked up the cliff for any sign of the beast. It appeared to be gone and so was the rope he used to get down there in the first place.

He wasn't sure how he was going to get down. He survived the attack, but now can he survive the escape? Rowan looked down over the side of the small cliff, trying to figure out how exactly was he going to get down.

He noticed that on the left side of the cliff it sloped at such an angle that he might be able to climb down.

The rocks on the slope looked very loose. He'd have to be careful climbing down and keep his body close to the slope due to the steepness. It only went down like that for a short way until it became too steep to climb down. He would have to scoot across to the further end where he could try to climb down further.

Rowan scooted to the edge and carefully slid his body down the slope, hugging the side of the cliff wall with his body.

Already some small rocks were starting to tumble down from under him. He even slid slightly when some of the loose dirt on the cliff wall broke free.

He tried to dig his fingers deep into the slope to prevent sliding down any further as he continued to gingerly descend down the side.

The descent was thus far going as planned as he continued to make his way down. Just as he was nearing the ledge where he had planned to shift over, a rock came loose under him and caused him to slide down.

He tried to stop himself from sliding anymore by digging his fingers into the dirt and pressing his body against the hillside. His efforts were all to no avail as he became the center of a mini rock slide that dragged him down with it.

Rowan slide down cliff's ledge and went over the side, tumbling in the air towards the ground beneath him.

As he headed toward the ground, the top of a pine tree broke his fall, but it broke as well. He tumbled into the next one which also broke. He bounced to the next and then to the next as he fell and tumbled his way to the ground through the tree. Each limb either broke from his falling on it or bent down, rolling him to the side to drop down even further.

He fell through the tree crashing limb to limb

until with a loud and dull thud, Rowan finally hit the ground...hard.

He hurt from just about every place on his body as he feebly gasped for air. The wind had been knocked out of him so times on the way down he almost wasn't sure how to breathe again.

The tree had beaten him to a pulp, but it had broken his fall and saved his life. He was alive and that surprised even him.

Rowan rested on the ground for a few minutes, reflecting upon his luck on escaping the dead walker and then surviving the fall. That and the fact he couldn't move yet and was still trying to catch his breath again.

He was definitely lucky, but for how long.

After a few minutes Rowan finally rolled to his side and looked around. He was in a ravine on the mountain side. He tried to figure out which way to go.

He prided himself on having a pretty good sense of direction and he did know 'about' which way he needed to go to get back to the longhouse. But he'd never seen this place before.

Below him, he could see where the ravine led down. It was not as steep as before, although it was much more rocky.

It was different down here than it had been up where the dead walker was. There was a sense of peacefulness. He could hear the birds chirping and it didn't seem as 'dead' and strange. Plus the intense smell of rot wasn't present.

Rowan stood up and steadied himself. He was bruised and hurt everywhere, but he was still able to move on his own. Surprisingly, nothing was broken.

He began making his way down the ravine, being mindful of the loose rocks as to not stumble and hurt himself any more than he already was. He knew he needed to head West, but the ravine was taking him in a more northerly direction. He figured that once he got lower and more off the mountainside, he'd be able to better recognize where he was and be able to navigate his way back a bit better.

After walking a bit he came near to the end of the ravine where it leveled out on the hillside. Rowan began to veer his path more west.

He tried to stay as much as he could in the clearing in hopes of recognizing something that would lead his way. Unfortunately, so far nothing stood out as familiar to him.

He continued to walk and stay as westwardly as he could, trying to prevent entering the forest as much as possible. He foolishly lost his ax when he threw it at the undead thing and was unarmed. He didn't want to become prey to wolves or anything else that lived in the forest. He also heard stories of hidden things that lived in the forest, but never believed them. He always assumed that they were tales meant to keep children from straying into the woods.

He was a believer in those stories now.

At this point Rowan had been walking for most of the day and he knew he'd gone too far North. When they had initially gone up the mountain through the woods trying to find the sheep, it had only taken them a little over half a day to reach the location where the beast had been.

Rowan could tell that there was only another hour or two before the sun would set. This was not good. He had no supplies, weapons, or anything and was on the edge of a forest. He'd have to make a decision as to what to do for the night.

Additionally, he didn't feel very safe, not because of the wolves that he was sure would be coming out for their nightly hunt, but he couldn't shake the feeling that he was being watched. He felt it all day.

As he ventured further, he spotted a hollow in the ground under a tree. It would serve as a good place to hide during the night and offered some protection. At least he believed it would. He figured that he could crawl in and close it off with some branches to conceal it.

Rowan set to work immediately while he still had light to work in. He first checked the hallow to make sure nothing else was in there. There was always the chance that it was the home of some kind of wildlife and the last thing he wanted to do was crawl in and have a pack of animals angry and attacking him.

He picked up a rock and threw it into the hole and listened.

Nothing.

It was too dark in the hole for him to see inside. So he picked up another rock and threw it in.

Nothing.

He grew more confident that the hole was probably unoccupied. Rowan picked up a dead branch and put one end inside of it and shook it around in hopes of disturbing and running out anything inside. He wanted to make certain it was empty before he actually crawled in it himself.

Still nothing.

Satisfied that the hole was probably empty, he crawled inside of it.

First he slowly lowered in his legs, hoping nothing would bite them. Then he lowered the rest of his body down and entered the hallow. Once inside the hole he felt around in the hole with his hands for anything.

It was empty and he felt confident of it now. This will serve as his hide-away for the night.

He climbed back out of the hole and gathered some brush to hide the hollow's opening while he occupied it for the night. The dead limb he used to see if anything was in the hole, he'd keep with him as a club. Just in case he had to defend himself inside the hole.

He set up brush in front the hole to conceal it. After that he secured himself inside the hollow for the night. He finished securing his hide-away just in time before he ran out of sunlight. Rowan laid in the hole facing the opening and clinched the dead limb. It wasn't long before his exhausted, bruised body had overcome him and he fell asleep.

Chapter 6 - An Interesting Night

Rowan woke up to the sound of rustling leaves. The sound was comes from somewhere near him outside of the hole. He opened his eyes and looked out into the darkness trying to see what was out there. While his eyes were still slowly adjusting, he heard the sound of leaves crunching from a foot step.

Something was definitely something out there.

He heard more leaves rustling and heavy foot steps outside in the darkness. His heart began to pound at the thought that it might be the dead walker looking for him. He had no where to go. His hide-away for the night had now become his trap.

However. he didn't smell the nauseating dead rotting flesh smell as he did before when the dead walker was near.

There was a smell though, but this smell was different. It smelled of rancid dried sweat and dirt. It was more of a 'nasty-dirty' smell than a 'rancid-rotten' smell. It most likely wasn't the dead walker, but what was it?

Rowan was still clinching onto his stick and peering into the darkness outside of his hole. He could hear it, but couldn't see what it was. He started moving forward in order to sneak a peek outside of the hole to see what was out there making the noise. As he crept forward, he heard it snort as it continued taking heavily steps outside.

It was definitely something big, he could also feel the ground slightly shake with each step it took. Rowan's curiosity outweighed his cautiousness. He had to see what was outside of the hole.

Just as he was about the scoot forward to peer outside of the hole, he heard something softly whisper behind him say, "don't."

Rowan paused for a second. Although a bit stunned, he wasn't sure he'd actually heard anything.

"Don't move. Don't make a sound or it will find you and kill you," he heard it whisper again in the darkness behind him.

Horror crawled through Rowan when he realized the whispering was coming from inside the hole behind him. Whoever or whatever was whispering to him was in the hole with him, concealed in the darkness.

Just before he was about to turn to look and try to see what was behind him talking, he sees the thing outside walk past the opening of the hollow he was in.

Whatever it was, it was huge. Rowan was only able to see the lower parts of its legs from just above the knees down in the darkness. It had to be at least three times taller than a tall man, maybe more. He could see that it had huge hairy feet and hairy legs.

It must be a giant, Rowan thought. He'd never seen a man that big in his life. He heard the stories of giants and of the gods battling them. It was believed that they were all extinct, killed in god's wars against the giants. Occasionally there was rumor of someone seeing one. But those reports were usually after several horns of mead and never taken seriously.

The ground slightly shook as it walked past Rowan's hidden hallow. He could only sit there in the darkness of his hole fearfully hoping that it didn't find him. But something was in the hole with him. Whatever was in the hole with him wasn't threatening him, but he couldn't be sure if he was actually safe or not from it.

For the moment, the large man-like beast outside of the hole seemed to be a greater of the dangers to him. He didn't know what to do, but he figured his chances were better if he just stayed in the hole and remain quiet.

Rowan sat quietly hidden in the hollow as he listened to the large thing outside slowly walk away into the distance.

It was then when he heard whomever occupied the hollow with him say, "I think it's gone now."

Rowan was scared. He knew that no other human being would have been able to fit in the hole with him. At least not without laying on him or being real close next to him. Either way, he felt nobody next to him. Whatever it was, it was very small.

"Who are you?" demanded Rowan.

"My name is Tom," he heard it say in the darkness, "Tom Tay."

"Listen," Tom began, "Stay here through the rest of the night and try not to make a sound. Only come out when you can see that the sun has risen. When you exit this hallow, you will see some white flowers that have grown on a rock. Head in the direction and stay on that course. You will have to pass through the forest, but you will be safe as long as you wait for daylight. Later in the day, follow the sun though the

76

forest and when you emerge, you will recognize that you are not too far from your village."

"Wait, how do you know who I am and where my village is?" questioned Rowan. "Who are you and what was that thing out there?"

"I told you. My name is Tom, we will meet again and that thing out there was a troll." Tom replied. "A rather hunger one at that," he added.

"A troll!" Rowan said shocked. "I thought those things weren't real."

"I am surprised you still don't believe in things after what you seen come out of that mound. Dead things aren't suppose to come back either, but it chased you over a cliff didn't it. There are many unseen things out there, both good and bad. Sadly, most are bad. Well, at least for humans like yourself" Tom said.

"We will meet again, follow my instructions and you will be fine. For now, I must go."

Before Rowan could say anything, the small thing that called itself Tom ran out of the hole. So fast that Rowan only got a tiny glimpse of it in the darkness.

It was like a tiny human, probably no taller than house cat. But it was dark and Rowan really didn't get a good look at it as it ran out of the hole. Before

he knew it, it was gone. Interestingly, the being that
called itself 'Tom' exited the hole and disappeared
without really making a sound. Tom Tay seemed to
be extremely light footed and very fast.

Chapter 7 - Through the Forest

Rowan did what Tom had advised him to do and stayed in the hollow for the rest of the night without making a sound. After learning that trolls were real and having one nearly discover him, sleep was out of the question. So Rowan kept a vigilance inside the hole until he seen the sun rise and announce that morning had come.

Emerging from the hollow that had been his refuge, Rowan followed Tom's instructions and entered the forest. He immediately found a rock which was covered in the white flowers of moss heather.

Rowan putting the morning sun to his back tread his way through the forest heading west. He still had the stick that he had armed himself with during the night and used it as a walking stick. His body was beaten and he hadn't really rested for a few days. On top of that, he hadn't eaten. He felt weak from injury, fatigue, and hunger.

Suddenly he remembered the honey biscuit he had wrapped up and tucked inside his shirt.

Rowan stopped walking and dropped his club/walking stick on the ground. He quickly reached inside his shirt and felt around for the biscuit. It wasn't there!

He pulled his shirt out and shook it, hoping the wrapped honey biscuit would drop.

It was gone! He must have lost it when he fell off the cliff and through that tree.

Disappointed, Rowan fixed his shirt and looked ahead. He could see what looked like golden flowers. It was the tell tale signs of what was probably chanterelle.

He picked up his stick and began walking towards them. As he approached them, he could already smell their fruity aroma. These were definitely the yellow edible mushrooms he was hoping they'd be.

Rowan rejoiced. He wasn't out of options yet.

His stomach gurgled as he picked them. Having no means to make a fire and cook them, he ate them raw. To his surprise, they were very peppery in contrast to their sweet smell and also very chewy. He wasn't sure if it were safe to eat them raw, but his hunger overrode his wisdom and he gobbled them down.

He only ate enough of them until his hunger subsided, but already his stomach felt ill and he wondered if he should have eaten them after all.

He knew some mushrooms were poisonous and hoped he hadn't been foolish and allowed his hunger to seal his doom. His stomach was upset, but he wasn't really ill from it. Although not at his best, he felt confident that he'd be okay and proceeded with his trek through the forest.

As he walked through the forest, he made sure he kept his direction true by checking the sun now and again. Because of the mushrooms, he did have to stop on occasion to let his stomach settle. He wasn't really ill and he didn't feel nauseated, but he sure felt uneasy.

It was when he had stopped to lean against his walking stick and let his stomach settle that he heard something rustling behind him.

His heart beat began to quicken as soon as he thought of the troll. Remembering the tales he'd heard about trolls, he was sure they never came out in the daylight. Daylight was bad for them, he couldn't remember why, but he remembered that trolls absolutely could not come out in the day light. The sun did something very bad to them.

Because the Sun was out, it most likely wasn't a troll. But something was there.

Cautiously he slowly turned and looked behind him.

Nothing was nothing there.

At least he didn't see anything, that didn't mean nothing was there. Maybe it was that wee Tom Tay character that had helped him avoid the troll last night.

He decided to call out, "Tom? Is that you? Tom Tay!"

Rowan listened for any kind of response, but got none. Save for the occasional bird or breeze blowing through the trees above, he heard nothing.

Feeling confident it was just his imagination, Rowan continued walking through the forest. It wasn't but a few moments later that he heard it again. It wasn't just a rustling of leaves that he heard, but the sounds of footsteps.

They didn't sound like those made by a human. They were to soft and sounded like they had sort of a leap to them. Like how a deer would trot, but with only two legs.

84

Rowan stopped again and turned towards the sound to look and listen, but again he seen and heard nothing.

Something was in the forest following him, he was certain that. He scanned the trees around where he figured the sound had came from. Looking for any sign of something hiding in the foliage.

As he looked around, he couldn't help reflecting on the fact that there certainly seemed to be many things in the forest that were out to get him. He couldn't believe it. All the stories he'd heard about the various creatures living in the woods. Stories that he thought were just meant to keep children from wandering off in the forest and getting lost. Stories about things that actually existed after all.

After a moment of listening so intently that he hardly breathed and seeing absolutely nothing, Rowan decided to proceed. This time with a quicker pace. Whatever it was, wasn't going to show itself apparently. It was best just to get through the forest as quickly as possible.

The Sun had passed over him and he was still making its way west. According to Tom's directions, it shouldn't be that much further.

Quite frankly, he couldn't wait to get out of the forest. The drab life of a blacksmith's thrall wasn't so bad after all, considering everything that's happened. At least as a thrall he rarely had to venture out into the wilderness where things we set on killing him.

At that point it dawned on him about the blacksmith and his son. They were dead. He wouldn't be able to return to life as it was before. What was to become of him? Who in their right mind would believe him when he told them what had happened. He knew he wouldn't believe such a story himself if he'd heard it being told. Especially such a tail told by a thrall. They would suspect that he'd murdered his master in an attempt to escape his servitude. Surely he would be put to death for murder.

Rowan's wandering mind was quickly silenced when he heard the footsteps again. It was like a trot and it was now to his left. He noticed that he was at a half run himself. He didn't even notice his pace had quickened, but it had. He also noticed that his heart was also pounding.

He continued his pace and pretended not to notice the trotting off to the left of him. He tried not look in its direction, for fear it would try to hide out of sight from him again.

He did his best to look in the corner of his eye, without turning his head to try and see what it was.

In the back of his mind, he was hoping it would just be a deer, but over the last couple days he'd learned that it would be expecting to much for it to be something normal and ordinary. Besides, there was nothing ordinary about a deer trotting beside a human anyways.

Rowan did finally catch a glimpse of it. He caught a short quick glimpse of what appeared to be a woman with long flowing curly blonde hair. He also thought she was nude as well, but wasn't sure.

Before he got a good look at her she disappeared in the trees and was out of his sight once again.

He stopped abruptly in his tracks and looked in the direction that she'd gone. He could still hear her moving through the trees. It sounded like she was trotting off instead of running. But his imagination and perhaps because of the mushrooms he'd eaten were playing tricks on him. He was also fairly sleep deprived as well.

The sound faded off and Rowan took a quick look around him to make sure nothing else was there.

Feeling satisfied that he was once again alone and perhaps the trotting was nothing but a deer with his mind playing tricks on him. It may have been something else, but it didn't matter. He set off again to get out of the forest.

His stomach had finally settled down and his shaken nerves had given him a sense of renewed energy. His pace at a half jog. Getting out of the forest was now his priority.

Rowan had kept this pace up for quite a bit until he began feeling tired from it. Which was acceptable, because he could see a clearing ahead. It meant that he was about to come out of the forest. He was relieved.

Even though he was exhausted, he decided not to rest and continued walking. He was determined to get to the clearing and out of the forest. However, as he started walking towards the clearing he heard the sound of giggling behind him.

Rowan stopped walking and just stood there frozen in his tracks.

As he stood there motionless, listening, he heard it again. It was a female's giggle.

Reluctantly Rowan turned around in the direction he heard the giggling coming from and was surprise to see the face of a woman peering at him from behind a tree.

It was the woman he thought he'd seen trotting past him earlier that had disappeared in the woods.

Although he wasn't sure if he'd been seeing things or not earlier, he was sure of what he seen now.

It was her. She had the same long curly blond hair that fell over her shoulders. Her hair covered her shoulders and the rest of her body was hidden behind a tree. Rowan still wasn't sure if she was nude or not, but her shoulders and arms were bare.

She just smiled as she looked at him and then giggled again.

Bewildered, Rowan just looked at her with his mouth agape. She was beautiful, perhaps the most beautiful woman he'd ever seen. That is, of what he could see of her.

Rowan relaxed his guard a bit realizing that he must be near the village and this was just someone he'd never seen before. Maybe a visitor from another village perhaps. He was just about to ask her who she was and if he was near the village when he spotted something most peculiar.

On the other side of the tree that she was hiding behind, he swore he seen a tail swish. It looked like a cow's tail or something similar. It had swished and then was quickly hidden behind the tree again.

She reached her arm out and beckoned him to come nearer as she giggled again at him.

Temptation was overwhelming, he couldn't help feeling extremely attracted to her and he didn't know why. But he hadn't forgotten about everything else that had happened so far and thought better of it. She seemed friendly, but that didn't mean anything out here in the forest. Besides, why was she hiding behind the tree? It could be a trap, so he decided to play it cool and said to her in the most polite way he could.

"My apologies, but I am in a bit of a hurry. I hope to see you again soon though."

He didn't feel right about this, so he quickly turned and walked away. Rowan kept his quickened pace the rest of the way out of the forest. He did, however, carefully listen as he walked to make sure she wasn't following him.

His mind raced as he walked briskly out of the forest. She was beautiful and probably naked, but why was she naked and why was she hiding herself behind the tree? And was that a tail he seen flicking behind her? He swore he'd seen a tail swish behind her.

She didn't seem to be following him, but he didn't hear her run off either. He wasn't going to take the chance of looking behind him to make sure she was gone. His instincts told him to not look back, just keep going and don't stop.

To his joy, he reached the edge of forest and had entered the clearing. There was a ridge line ahead, so Rowan decided to take a quick look and see if he could figure out where he was.

When Rowan reached the summit of the ridge, he seen the fjord below and recognized the hillside. He wasn't too far away. He knew where he was now and which way to go to get the rest of the way back.

Chapter 8 - The Inquisition

After a couple more hours of trekking down the hill side and through a few patches of woods, Rowan finally made it to the outskirts his village. The blacksmith's longhouse where he belonged was located on the other side of the village.

He paused overlooking the village and pondered how to best proceed. He would need to inform the Blacksmith's family as to what had happened to the Blacksmith and his son. Jarl Erling, the leader of the village, would have to be informed as well.

But he didn't know exactly how to handle that. As a thrall, he had no equal voice as did the Karls, the freemen. His master was the one that would speak to the Jarl on his behalf if it were ever needed.

But his master was no longer alive. It would be best to speak to Gwenda, the blacksmith's wife, and have her speak with the Jarl.

Rowan figured it would be best to go around the village settlement and make his way to the blacksmith's long house. This way he could avoid everyone else and not have to explain himself.

Satisfied on his solution, he began making his way around the village. He tried to keep just inside the wood line and out of sight.

Unfortunately his plans were ruined when he heard, "Thrall! Where's your master the Blacksmith?"

Someone had called out to him. Already, his plans have been foiled.

Rowan stopped dead in his tracks, turned and looked in the direction of the voice. He recognized the man, it was one of the Karls from the village. Apparently he was in the woods chopping firewood and Rowan didn't notice him while he was walking through.

Rowan just stood there surprised and looked at him without saying anything. The man was sitting on a felled tree that he'd apparently just chopped down and was quietly taking a rest.

"I asked you a question thrall, where's your master?" the Karl demanded.

Rowan's heart began to race, he didn't know how to answer. The very direct question he was intentionally trying to avoid until he'd at least spoken to Gwenda was just now presented to him.

The Karl angrily stood up while holding his chopping ax and demanded more forcefully, "Answer me thrall!"

Rowan looked down upon the ground and quietly said, "he was killed on the mountain by a beast."

The man gave a doubting lift of his eyebrow and stood there for a moment thinking as he looked at Rowan up and down.

Finally he said, "come with me" and motioned Rowan to walk with him towards the village.

Rowan obediently turned and began walking towards the village. He had no choice really. If he refused the demand of the Karl, one of the village's freemen, he would have been cut down by the man's ax.

There was a difference between a thrall, whom was property, and that of a freeman. It would not of been considered murder to kill a thrall. There would only be an obligation to pay the thrall's owner for damage to their property. It was no different than killing a cow or breaking a tool and then having to pay the owner the amount for replacement.

They walked the whole way without saying a word. Rowan walking in front with the Karl behind him, holding his ax over his shoulder. They walked this way until they reached the village and continued towards the center. They gathered an occasional curious look from the villagers that took noticed them.

They stopped when they reached the village center where the Jarl's Hall was located. This was were Jarl Erling resided, although Rowan himself had never been inside. He'd been to the village center many times and even to the Jarl's Hall, but was always told to wait outside. The Hall was a place for freemen.

However, this time Rowan got to go in and see what it looked like inside for the first time. The Karl who led Rowan there had pushed him inside while he told him to go in.

Rowan stumbled in the doorway and nearly tripped and fell flat on his face. As he entered he was momentarily blinded. It took a moment for Rowan's eyes to adjust to the lighting inside.

He was surprised by the hall's size. It looked even bigger from the inside than it did from the outside. The design was very different than the typical longhouse. It was much larger and more open to accommodate a larger group of people.

There were three great fire pits in the center of the Jarl's Hall. Each fire pit had heavy wooden tables and benches lined on each side of them. Along the walls were additional rows of heavy tables that also had benches on each side. On the opposite end of the hall there was a seat that was raised up above the others.

Rowan could see Jarl Erling seated at this raised chair with some of his armed House Karls at guard on either side of him.

Rowan knew what the Jarl looked like, he'd seen him on numerous occasions when the Jarl requested items to be made by the blacksmith. Bjord had crafted many things for the Jarl on many occasions.

The Karl that brought Rowan into the Jarl's Hall grabbed him by the iron collar that he wore around his neck and used it to lead him to the Jarl.

When they were in front of the Jarl, the karl pulled Rowan down by the iron collar and commanded, "on your knees thrall!"

Rowan obeyed, keeping his eyes lowered and knelt down before the Jarl, whom was looking at them with great curiosity.

"Jarl Erling, my lord, I found this thrall outside the village. I asked him where his master was and he claims that his master had been killed by a wild beast."

The Jarl nodded without saying a word.

The karl added, "we haven't seen the blacksmith in a couple days, I suspect this thrall has killed his master and his son."

Neutral faced, Jarl Erling quietly looked at Rowan for a few moments before turning to one of his guards standing next to him and ordered, "bind him."

The guard stepped forward and took Rowan's hands behind him and bound them with leather lashings. After tying the binding, he lifted Rowan up by his arm and pulled him up to his feet.

The guard then guided Rowan back near the fire that was in front of the Jarl and pulled him back down to his knees and stood behind him.

As Rowan was being watched by one the Jarl's guards, the Jarl instructed another guard to "fetch the blacksmith's household."

The guard turned and expeditiously exited the hall.

Rowan remained there on his knees facing the Jarl with his head bowed down and hands bound behind him. He was not sure of what was to become of him. This was definitely not a good predicament to be in and now he questioned his decision to return.

The Jarl's Hall gradually began filling up with men from the village. They were curious as to what was going on. Rowan could hear the murmur of them speaking amongst themselves. After a few minutes, a man stepped forward Rowan recognized as Thorn, the brother of his master Bjord the blacksmith.'

Thorn spoke before the hall to Jarl Erling, "I demand justice for my brother and his son Sven. Justice that this thrall be put to death for his crimes of murder."

Rowan was horrified when heard this. It was exactly what he feared might happen. He did not do anything wrong, but how in the world would he prove it.

The karl that brought Rowan in, which Rowan had now learned was named Oleg, quickly countered by saying, "I take claim to this thrall."

"How do you have the right the take claim of the thrall?" contested Thorn.

"I take claim for finding the thrall that was trying to escape after having slayed his master. He no longer had a master and belongs to the first to claim him." explained Oleg.

"That is nonsense." protested Thorn. "The thrall, and any other property belonging to Bjorn, would be passed to his heirs."

"There aren't any legal heirs, as the thrall has claimed the blacksmith and his son, his only son, are now dead. Without any heirs, the property is up for grabs." Oleg pointed out.

"That is not the only heir and I am his brother!" blasted Thorn, "besides, the murderer will be put to death for his crimes and not claimed by anyone!"

At this point Jarl Erling stood up and called for the men to settle down. He stepped down from his throne seat and calmly said, "we're not even sure yet if Bjorn and his son are even dead. Let us hear from his household first to verify."

This paused the two men of their bickering. The Jarl turned around and stepped back up on his throne and sat in his chair. He motioned to one of the guards that was standing off to the side and leaned in to whisper something in his ear. When the Jarl sat back, the man quickly headed out the door of the hall on some unknown task.

The chatter in the hall gradually became louder and louder as more men continued to come in and inquire as to what was going on. It was then when the blacksmith's wife, Gwenda, showed up along with her mother Helga that the Hall began to quieten.

The men in the hall fell silent as Gwenda and Helga made their way past them. Gwenda was helping her mother and supporting her as they walked to the end of the Hall in front of Jarl Erling.

Gwenda stood before the Jarl, still helping her mother along. She looked briefly at Rowan with a puzzled look before facing the Jarl and asking, "my lord, why have you summoned us to your Hall?"

"Woman, where is your husband and son?" asked Jarl Erling.

"My lord, they have gone into the forest up the mountainside a couple days ago. They left with our thrall, the three of them."

"A couple days ago with your thrall? Why did they go into the forest?"

"My lord, we had been awakened in the middle of the night by a loud screech and the sound of our livestock panicking. Our sheep were the most panic stricken and they ran out of their pens into the house until they finally ran through the door and escaped outside. We never seen what was causing them to become so afraid, but our thrall said that a strange cat had chased them."

"A strange cat?" inquired Jarl Erling.

"Yes, our thrall claimed that there was a cat that woke him up by sitting on his chest trying to crush him him. He said when he tried to get the cat off of him, it went after our livestock."

She briefly paused, looking around at the faces of the men in the Hall. Many had puzzled looks and were shaking their heads in disbelief.

"Yes, I understand. Please, continue." Jarl Erling encouraged.

"Well,.. we ran outside to fetch the frightened sheep, but they already ran up the hill and went into the forest. We could hear them in the darkness screaming as they ran. It was too dark to try to find them in the night, so my husband decided to track them in the morning. When morning came and before anything else had been done that day, my husband, my son, and our thrall set out to find the sheep and bring them back."

"And that was the last time you had heard from any of them?"

"Yes, that was the last time we had heard from any of them. Until now."

"Until now?" Jarl Erling asked.

"Yes, my lord, until now,." She turned and

motioned towards Rowans. "I see our thrall has returned. But what of my son and my husband? It has been three days now."

There were repeats of this question made angrily by several of the men in the Jarl's Hall that had been listening.

At this point Oleg yelled. "The thrall must be put to death for murder. The blacksmith's household deserves justice!"

There were shouts of agreement from several other men in the Hall. Rowan could feel a lump in his throat as concern for his life began to grow even more.

Things began getting louder, the Jarl had to stand up and raised his hand to quieten the men in the Hall. Once the Hall became quiet again he looked down upon Rowan and said, "tell us thrall Rowan, what happened to your master?"

Oleg barked in, "who cares what the thrall has to say, he..."

"Silence!" demanded the Jarl before Oleg could finish what he was saying. "We don't even know what happened. There is only speculation at this point. We will give him a chance to tell us what happened and then we will check his story."

Looking back at Rowan, Jarl Erling again asked, " tell us what happened when you went looking for the sheep? Tell us everything that happened."

Everyone in the Hall quietened at this point to listen as Rowan told his story.

"Like Gwenda had said, I woke up in the middle of the night because I was having trouble breathing. When I woke up, I found a cat sitting in my chest staring at me. It wasn't a normal cat, because it was as heavy as a man. Its weight was crushing my chest and I couldn't breathe. It kept getting heavier and heavy and seemed to also get bigger and bigger."

Someone from the hall shouted in protest, "this is utter nonsense." He was silenced by 'hushes' from the rest of the men in the Hall before the Jarl needed to bother intervening.

Rowan continued. "The cat had me trapped under its weight and I couldn't breathe. When I tried to get it off of me by jerking my body, it howled and jumped off of me. That's when it chased after the sheep. It screeching the whole time it chased them. It scared the sheep until they ran out of the longhouse and into the darkness of the forest."

Gwenda and her mother Helga confirmed all this by nodding their heads in agreement when the Jarl looked at them.

Rowan recapitulated. "We left first thing the very next morning to track the sheep. We tracked them up the mountain to a hidden burial mound that we discovered."

"A hidden burial mound? What?" Questioned the Jarl.

"Yes my lord, it was when we were investigating the burial mound that it all happened.

"What happened?"

"We were attacked by a large creature."

"A bear?" Someone among the men of the hall called out.

"No, worse. It was some kind of dead beast. Bigger than a man and stronger than a bear. It killed Bjord and then it killed Sven. I escaped by running and climbing down a cliff. I got down the other side side and hid in the forest."

"So you ran like a coward and left them to die."

"No, they were already dead." Rowan bravely protested. "We were unable to inflict any kind of damage to it. Except..."

"Except what?"

"Except when I was able to put Bjord's ax into its back. It appeared to burn it."

"The ax burned it? What do you mean, how can an ax burn anything?"

"My lord, when the ax was embedded in its back, I could see smoke coming from the wound and it struggled trying to remove it. It looked like the ax really hurt it."

"It you were hurting it, how come you didn't slay it?" Inquired the Jarl.

"I didn't have a weapon any longer and knew I would not be able to kill it. Now alone and disarmed, I did the only thing I could do. I ran."

"You ran?"

"I ran, but the beast gave chase and was unnaturally fast. I knew I wouldn't be able to outrun it, so I took the rope we brought and climbed down the side of the cliff. That was how I escaped it. I spent the next day finding my way back. That was when Oleg found me. I was on my way to the blacksmith's house to inform his wife what had happened."

There was much debate and loud murmuring going on amongst everyone in the Hall at that point.

Oleg stepped forward plead to the Jarl, "my lord, you don't believe this thrall's story do you? It's obvious that he has made up a tale to cover up his crime."

A raspy voice broke in from behind everyone near the main door. It was the settlement's lawspeaker, Alvis the wise. The old man had quietly come in and had been listening to the whole story.

"There may be truth to the thrall Rowan's tale." He said in a dry raspy voice as he made his way to the other side of the Hall through the other men with the assistance of his staff aiding him as he walked.

"What say you lawspeaker." asked the Jarl when the old man had came in front of him. He motioned one of the guards to fetch a chair for the old man to seat himself.

After the lawspeaker sat down, he spoke again saying, "there has been talk of something dreadful lurking in the mountain side for a few years. Stories that men have told when they ventured too far up the hill when hunting."

Someone in the crowd piped in stating, "those are just tales!"

The lawspeaker nodded and said, "yes tales they are, but none the less they all seem to say the same thing. What we know of the dead walkers is they do have the power to shape shift into a small creature and it has also been said that they will try to crush someone in their sleep by growing larger and heavier."

"Sorcery!" yelled someone from the crowd.

"Perhaps." affirmed the lawspeaker, "but we don't really know what they are. I haven't heard of a dead walker since I was a young lad. They called them Draugs."

"That was in a an age before time itself!" joked someone loudly from the crowd, making a reference to the lawspeaker's age. Laughter erupted in the crowd.

The lawspeaker when silent upon that joke, he didn't find it funny at all. After they got their laughs out, the Jarl spoke and said, "we will send a group of men to investigate the burial mound and see if what the thrall claims is true."

There was murmur of protest about this until someone stepped forward and said, "this is nonsense, there are no monsters on the mountain. This thrall killed his master and his master's son and needs to be put to death for it."

There was a load roar of agreement from many men in the Hall with this statement.

The Jarl had to once again quieten the Hall and said, "we will investigate this matter by sending a group of men to the location. The thrall will lead them to the mound. If there is any proof of wrongdoing by the thrall, he will be brought back to this hall and be put to death in accordance to our laws."

There were a few men shaking their heads, disagreeing to the Jarl's decision. They otherwise had no choice but to accept it. The Jarl added to this by stating, "however, if there is any truth to this, then the thrall will be cleared and we shall have to do something about the creature."

Most of the men agreed to this resolution, however many exclaimed their protests because they didn't believe in such a creature and that thrall was doing nothing but creating a story to save his own hide.

Jarl Erling then called for volunteers. "I need some men to go up the mountain. They will be guided by the thrall first thing tomorrow morning to investigate if there is any truth to his story."

Nobody stepped forward and the Hall became silent.

"Why aren't there any brave men to step forward, I thought none of you believed in such creatures. After all, this thrall that I have repeated heard some of you call a coward has faced this beast." Jarl Erling mocked.

Having their courage and honor now challenged, several men stepped up and proudly proclaimed that they'd go.

The Jarl took five of the Karls from the village wishing to volunteer and an additional three of his own guard of Housekarls to accompany them.

It was planned that they'd leave at sunrise and the thrall Rowan would guide them to the exact location in order to verify his story.

One of the Jarl's guards took Rowan to the corner of the great hall and attached a chain to the iron ring around his neck . He then fastened the other end of the chain to one of the Hall's support beams.

Rowan was given a meager meal of porridge by one of the Jarl's own thralls. Having not ate for a couple days, save a few raw wild mushrooms that made him feel a little ill, he was grateful for it.

The evening went on rather late as men were feasting on meats and drinking mead. Rowan obviously was not apart of this festivity and simply sat quietly in the corner with his back to the pole that he was chained to.

The past couple of days had overwhelmed him with exhaustion and it wasn't long until he fell asleep.

Chapter 9 - The Expedition

The morning came fast and Rowan felt much better after sleeping through the night. He slept through the entire noise of the evening with the merriment that took place in the Hall. His fatigue was too great to allow things such as being chained to a pole or the occasional item being tossed at him by someone in the Hall to be a bother to him.

He woke up to someone kicking his foot and telling him to 'get up.' Rowan looked up and seen that it was one of the Jarl's housekarls standing in front of him. He immediately got up to his feet. The Housekarl unchained him from the pole and removed the leather lashing that was used to bind his hands.

Rowan was relieved to have his hands untied. It was a bit painful, especially sleeping, to be bound like that. He rubbed his wrists to let the blood flow through them once again.

The Housekarl looked at Rowan and said, "I am not going to bother tethering you. I trust you won't run off." he said while patting the hilt of the sword that was hanging from his waist.

Rowan nodded.

The Housekarl led Rowan outside where the rest of the men had already gathered. It wasn't long before the men were ready to go.

They walked to the blacksmith's longhouse where Rowan showed them the path leading into the forest where the sheep had ran.

The men prepared themselves by putting on their battle gear. They wanted to make sure they were ready in case they were ambushed anywhere along the way. The Jarl's Housekarls wore spangenhelms with visors which made them look real intimidating. They also wore full chain mail shirts. Some of the karls that volunteered wore helms as well, but theirs weren't as good of quality as the ones worn by housekarls.

All the men had round wooden shields with iron shield bosses. Every shield was uniquely painted and different from one another. Some of the men had swords, some had spears, and a few carried battle axes. A couple of the men carried bows as well.

They were all equipped with smaller axes on

114

their belts, which was customary.

Except for Rowan, they were all well armed and prepared for anything that came their way.

Nevertheless, Rowan personally didn't think they were prepared for what was up on that hill. He knew his escaping was pure luck on his part and this time he was unarmed. Not that it mattered at this point. He knew he hurt it with the blacksmith's ax. There was something about the ax that hurt it when Sven's arrows didn't.

They walked into the forest and up the hill following the path led by Rowan. The trail left wasn't as prominent as it was before, so Rowan relied on memory and hope.

He hoped that he was taking them the right way. If he wasn't able to lead them to the mound where Bjord and Sven were killed, it would definitively be to his own doom.

They walked through the woods for a few hours until they came upon the remnants of the first sheep. This was the same one found by Bjord, but there wasn't much left of the sheep this time. Something had discovered it and had a feast. The only thing left of it were scattered bone and other parts. It was hard to tell it was even a sheep.

The sight of this pleased Rowan because it told

him that they were going the right way. This was a small glimmer of hope that he'd be able to prove his story and spare his life.

The men only paused briefly for a swig of mead then Rowan continued leading them up through the woods until they came to the spot where the other sheep was discovered.

Again it was obvious that wildlife had discovered the dead sheep and had a feast. There was only the sheep's head and a few bones left on this one. The remains reassured Rowan that he was still leading them in the right direction. His biggest fear of this whole expedition was going the wrong way and getting them lost.

As they continued further up the hill, the smell of decay began filling the air around them. It was a strangely strong and extremely rancid odor. One of the Karls that was carrying a spear was unable to tolerate it and lost his last meal when the smell got even stronger.

Apparently his stomach wasn't as strong as the rest of him.

A couple of the other men had on occasion gagged as well. Rowan wasn't sure if they were getting sick because of the smell alone or because of seeing the other man get sick, or a combination of both.

The smell of decay definitely had their attention. Rowan wasn't as bothered by the smell this time as he was before. He was more bothered by knowing what the smell belonged to. He knew the odor meant that the Dead Walker was near.

A few of the men were starting to get concerned and one of them said to the Housekarl leading the expedition, which Rowan learned was named Hakon. "What if the thrall isn't lying? Are we prepared for what we will find up there?"

Hakon answered, "we're prepared. We will make our stand no matter what is up there."

The rest of the men nodded in agreement, not wanting to reveal their own feelings of apprehension or show any sign of weakness.

They continued trekking up the hill as the smell grew stronger. A few of the men were now trying to cover their mouths in an attempt to not breath in the putrid scent and allow it to sicken them. It was hard for them not to feel like their stomachs weren't about to turn on them at any moment. In fact, Rowan thought the odor was a little bit stronger than it was the last time he'd been through there. Not wanting to alarm them any more than they already were, he kept that observation to himself.

Just as the eyes of some of the men were starting to water from the putrid smell, they reached the thicket brush that led to the cliff where Rowan climbed down when the creature chased him.

"This is where the sheep tracks ended." Rowan explained, "We figured that the sheep probably ran themselves through this bush and ran over the cliff on the other side. The hole through the bushes was much smaller."

He pointed to the now large hole through the bushes. "This is also where I escaped the creature."

The smaller hole Sven and Rowan had original crawled through was gone. The Draug had smashed its way through the bushes and made a large enough hole to walk to the ledge now.

Rowan noticed the rope he used to lower himself down was on the ground by the cliff's edge. He pointed out to the other men.

"There's the rope I used. It's still tied to the base of the bush root when I lowered myself down to escape the creature. It had grabbed the rope and tried to pull me up. That was when I was forced to let go and fall to the edge of a small cliff below."

One of the men picked up the rope and looked at it. After examining it he looked over the side of the cliff below and said, "you were very lucky to have landed on that small ledge."

Rowan agreed.

He turned and looked at the other men and said, "there was no other place to fall except to the rocks below. He was very lucky."

Rowan knew he was lucky, that is, except for now. He didn't feel so lucky anymore having to come back to where the creature was. That fact just dawned on him as he turned to where the brush was torn to the side leading up to the mound.

The thought of facing that creature again turned him pale. He absolutely did not want to go back up there. Especially to go back up there unarmed where the beast was probably waiting for them. But he had no choice. It was do this or face murder charges.

While the men were still examining where Rowan escaped, he turned and pointed to the path torn through the brush that was further up the hill.

"The mound where the creature came at us is through there. It's also where Bjord and Sven's bodies should still be."

"For your sake, you better be right."

"For all our sake, I hope I am wrong."

It was now obvious to the men that Rowan had been telling them the truth in the Jarl's Hall. They could see where the bushes and tree branches were torn away by something that was much larger than a man.

They walked up to where a path was torn through in the bushes and one of the men said to nobody in particular, "a bear perhaps?"

Another man responded by saying, "No, that was no bear."

Rowan pointed through the passageway and said, "the mound where the beast was is right through there, just on the other side of the path."

The men took on a new stance, they raised their shields and had their weapons at the ready for anything that would come through the torn passageway.

Rowan, being unarmed and unwilling, stood behind them.

He hoped the men would be able to successful battle the creature and kill it. But he had much doubt in that. He'd seen the beast in action and knew these men were no threat to it.

The passageway, which was barely wide enough for one man to pass through when Bjord, Sven, and Rowan had originally hacked their way through it, was now wide enough for three men to pass side by side. This was all thanks to the beast crashing its way through when it was chasing after Rowan.

The men grouped up three men wide, making a shield wall with their weapons poised as they carefully began stepping forward through the passage.

The remaining men packed behind them at the ready. The two men with bows each nocked an arrow and had them partially drawn back, ready to fire over the heads of the men in front of them.

Rowan tailed behind them a pace or two. He knew what laid ahead waiting and he was glad he was in the back of everyone. He didn't want to go through, but even though nobody told him to, he knew he had to pass through with them to the other side.

The men got through without incident and took up positions in front of the mound. They were not sure what to expect, except from what Rowan had told them had happened. The body of Bjord still laid where the beast had killed him.

Hakon walked over and investigated the body. The rest of the men looked on, not wanting to turn their backs to the mound. They now believed Rowan's story completely and were visibly shaken now.

Hakon knelt down and looked at Bjord's body, examining it for a few moments before standing back up.

"This was not done by any man. You can tell his body was crushed by something very large."

The Housekarl named Erik walked over by Hakon to inspect Bjord's body himself.

"That was done by something unnatural."

Hakon turned towards Rowan and asked, "where's the body of his son, Sven?"

"The creature threw his body over the side of the cliff." said Rowan as he pointed in the direction of the ledge, which was half concealed by brush.

The two men walked and looked over the side. They nodded at each other in agreement before returning to where the rest of the men were near the mound.

Hakon looked at Rowan and asked, "where did the creature come out from?"

Rowan looked at him and said, "I don't know. He was suddenly there upon us."

Incidentally, just as he said this, a mist began coming out from the burial mound and spreading in the immediate area around them.

"A mist just like this formed before it appeared!" cried Rowan in panic, remembering the mist now. He had forgotten about the mist.

Hakon lifted up his shield and yelled out to the rest of the men, "Shield Wall!"

The men assembled next to each other tightly and formed a shield wall by overlapping their shields together side by side. They held their weapons at the ready above their shields.

Rowan was greatly impressed by witnessing the disciple in their formation. His people were a warfaring folk and trained for battle their entire lives. It wasn't a thrall's place to be armed beyond that of a small ax carried on the belt, which was mainly used for utility reasons, but he's had the opportunity many times to help Sven train and learned how to form a shield wall.

In this case, however, Rowan stood behind his armed escort.

The mist grew thicker around them as did the putrid smell of death and decay in the air. It was a smell nobody could ever get accustomed to.

The two men with bows pulled back their draw strings, ready to fire their arrows immediately at the first sign of anything.

When the mist grew too thick to see through was
when they were startled by the ear piercing screech
of the dead walker suddenly appearing behind them.

The men on the shield wall quickly turned
around and tried to reform in the opposite direction.
They were too late. The massive angry beast, dark
blue in the color of decay, charged at them while
swinging its massive arms.

One of the swings knocked Rowan to the side,
causing him to tumble in the air. He hit the ground
hard and nearly rolled off the cliff edge it had
previously thrown Sven over just days ago.

The creature knocked both bowmen back as it
charged through them and caused them to misfire
their bows. Their arrows were sent harmlessly into
the air.

With a ferocious charge, it hit the line of men and
bashed three of them back several feet onto their
backs while they were trying to reform their shield
wall.

The creature then turned on one of the men
armed with a spear. It grabbed the weapon out of
his hands while smashing down on his head with his
fist. The injured man's legs gave way and he
slumped the ground dead. The creature's strength
was unnatural.

124

While the beast was attacking the man armed with a spear, another man behind it thrust his sword into the monstrosity's back and caused it to roar in pain. As he swung his sword for another hit, the fiend spun around and bashed him to the side with the back of its fist.

The hit caused the man to tumble feebly to the side as another man with an ax swung his weapon down upon the beast, hitting it in the shoulder. The beast angrily punched through that man's shield and caused it the shatter and spray wood splinters in the air. The beast hit him in the chest so powerfully that the man fell a couple feet backward. The ax wielder fell onto his back while spitting blood, dying from his chest being crushed from the powerful hit.

The men who had previously been knocked back, got up from the ground and jumped back into the fight. They swung their weapons, trying to hit the beast while at the same time trying not to get hit by the extremely powerful swings from its arms.

Rowan got up from the ground, being careful not to fall from the cliff he was almost swatted over and took a few steps forward before noticing Bjord's ax on the ground. It was hidden in the tall grass and was the very ax that Rowan sunk into the beast's back before making his escape previously. The creature must have pulled it free and tossed it there.

Rowan picked up Bjord's battle ax off the ground and slowly made his way to join the men fighting. He wasn't sure if it was really a good idea to fight in contrast to running.

The men kept getting knocked back as their hits on the beast appeared to be useless. Hakon was knocked back on the ground in front of Rowan. He was hit so hard that he had actually dropped his sword. His shield already had been shattered from one of the creature's strikes and discarded moments before. The Housekarl laid on the ground for a moment choking as he tried to reclaim the breath that had been knocked out of him by the hit.

Rowan stepped around Hakon and raised the ax he retrieved from the ground and began to approach the beast with the intent of striking it with all his might.

He was stopped short of his attack when he felt the Housekarl's hand grab his leg.

"No Thrall, it is useless. Run!"

Rowan lowered the ax and looked at him, not totally believing his words.

Hakon picked up his sword and rose to his feet and yelled, "it's useless men! Run! Run for your very lives!"

And with that retreating command, he lunged forward and grabbed one of the fighting men by the shoulder and yelled, "RUN!"

The remaining men turned and began running down the towards the path that lead them to the mound.

One man wasn't so lucky when the beast grabbed him from behind when he tried to run away.

The man swung feebly at the creature as it raised him above its head. This was enough to make Rowan join the rest of the men and run.

The beast threw the man he held at the group of others that were just now beginning to run and make their way through the passage. The beast managed to throw the man and hit two of the other men simultaneously and cause them to fall forward as they were attempting to run away. The beast was on them instantly before they could get back up on their feet.

Rowan ran with the Housekarl Hakon closely behind him. They had already passed through the bush path and continued to run as fast as they could down the hill.

Glancing back, Rowan could see that the creature already upon two of the last men that remained behind. It was one of the men that had been knocked down by the man that the beast had thrown at them and the man that was actually thrown, whom was miraculously still alive and fighting to the very end.

The other man that was knocked down had managed to get up to his feet and tore off running behind the rest of the men without looking back.

The Draug was beating the two men to death as the rest of the men continued to run down the hill. The man who had managed to get up and run after having being knocked down, still had his bow and turned to fire an arrow at the creature.

It was a solid shot and the arrow hit the beast in the eye. The dead walker roared with the most hideous howl that chilled everything that could hear it miles away right to the bone. Rowan was sure the village could hear it too. The beast's agonizing howl was that loud.

The creature grabbed the arrow that was stuck in its eye and began trying to pull it out. This was different than when he was hit by Sven's arrows. When the creature was hit by Sven's arrows, the dead walker ignored them. The arrow fired by the Karl seemed to really bother the monster and caused it great pain.

The archer fired another arrow into the creature with such great skill that he actually managed to hit the hand the creature was using to pull the first arrow out to his face and pinned its hand to its face. It was an incredible shot.

Both Rowan and Hakon momentarily stopped running to look in amazement.

The marksman's arrow hit made the creature extremely angry and it let out another ear piercing howl. It howled both from pain and from a furious anger never seen before.

It ripped its hand free with great force, leaving the arrow head and part of the shaft in its head with the first arrow still in its eye.

Everyone running had briefly considered turning back to fight the creature now that it appeared to be injured. But that notion was quickly thrown away when they seen the beast roar again and then leap a great distance. The beast landed directly on the archer, crushing him mercilessly.

Seeing the impossible great speed that the creature managed and its ability to leap great distances, even after being wounded, everyone knew they'd best keep running.

Which was what they all did. The remaining men continued to run down the hill with all their speed. This time not one person bothered looking back.

It was all they could do. Already losing most of the men immediately upon meeting this beast, it was clear that they would not be able to take down the beast. It was better to run and live to fight another day.

They continued to run as long as they could until exhaustion had taken over. They stopped running to rest for a moment and see if the beast still gave chase. It had been a few minutes since they heard the beast's howling in the distance.

It was safe to assume that they'd got ahead of it, but more in probably the beast just decided to not give chase. This was more probable due to the fact that the abomination was obviously faster than they were and it had proven: if it wanted to catch them, it could have easily.

They gathered together to catch their breath and see who had survived. There was only four of them left, including Rowan. Five armed veteran men had fallen to the creature and they don't even think they really even hurt it. They all witnessed how it reacted when the weapons struck it. They also knew they hurt it with the arrows as well, but it continued its attack as if unscathed by anything.

There was one thing beneficial to the whole predicament, at least in Rowan's eyes. He was no longer going to be accused of and executed for murder. Although his future was still in question, at least he wasn't going to be put to death for a crime he didn't commit.

There was still the fact that they'd lost over half the expedition, not mentioning finding an acceptable reason why they ran in the eyes of the other men in the village. It was considered a cowardly act to run away from any battle.

They gathered themselves and made one final look back to make sure the dead walker wasn't coming for them. Once satisfied that they weren't being pursued, they made their way back to the village.

Chapter 10 - Property

The expedition's survivors made their way back to the village. Word quickly passed of their arrival and many of the men in the village dropped what they were doing to gather in the Great Hall of the Jarl to find out what had happened. The fact that only four souls returned of the nine that had left, gathered much interest and curiosity.

It was close to dusk and there were already men gathered in the Hall that had been awaiting the return of the expedition. The four defeated men went into the Hall and all inside went quiet.

Silently the survivors walked past everyone as they made their way to the Jarl. Rowan gathered strange looks being that he was not bound and instead was carrying a battle ax. He was carrying Bjord's ax that he recovered near the mound.

Alvis the lawspeaker was already there and seated next to the Jarl.

As soon as they were in front of the Jarl, he questioned them.

"What happened? Where is the rest of the men that went with you?"

The Housekarl Hakon spoke softly stating, "Lord, all that the thrall Rowan had told us was the truth. We met the dead walker and I regret to report that we were defeated in battle. The other men have fallen."

The Hall immediately lit up with the loud voices of men as they demanded to know what had happened and why the Thrall dare enter the Jarl's Hall armed.

"Silence!" yelled the Jarl into the Hall, bringing everyone to a hushed quiet. Looking back at Hakon, he said, "tell me everything that has happened. Tell me why were you defeated?"

"My lord, we left this morning as planned. The thrall took us to the blacksmith's longhouse and showed us the trail where their sheep had ran in the darkness of night. We followed the trail through the woods and up the mountain for a distance. We had also found the remains of two different sheep along the way."

"Remains? What happened to them?"

"My lord, it appeared that animals had found their corpses and feasted upon them. The thrall informed us that the sheep were dead when they first followed the trail in search of them with the blacksmith. However, they were intact at that time. Wildlife had apparently discovered them since that time."

"I understand, continue."

"We continued following the path, led by the thrall, until we came to the location the thrall claimed he escaped the creature he described to us."

"Yes, were there any signs of Bjord or his son? Did you find their bodies?"

"Not at that specific location, my lord. There was a passageway torn through bushes that led to the burial mound that the thrall told us they had found. The bodies of Bjord the blacksmith and his son were there."

"Were you able to tell how they were killed? Were they murdered?"

"My lord, the bodies were mutilated by something that was not a man."

"Not a man? What do you mean?"

"My lord, we were met by the very monster that the thrall had said killed the blacksmith and his son."

Upon hearing the word, 'monster' the men in Hall began talking loudly amongst themselves again. They questioned the very existence of such a thing. A few even mocked the notion and laughed the moment they heard it.

Jarl Erling was growing very annoyed by everyone's inability to remain quiet enough in his Hall to allow him the ability to question Hakon, the Captain of his Housekarls.

"Silence!" yelled Jarl Erling as he stood up, red faced and angered. "I demand that this Hall remain quiet when I am trying to talk to this man and find out what happened or I will clear this Hall by force to quieted it!"

The Jarl's Housekarl guard present in the Hall immediately took to stepping forward at the ready for his command.

The men in the Hall quietened themselves, seeing the Jarl was becoming irritated and his guard ready to physically quieten them for him if need be.

Satisfied, Jarl Erling sat back down and then looked at Hakon and calmly said, "continue."

"Yes my lord, the monster or rather the dead walker. It was a huge beast, bigger than a man, bigger than a bear. It had dead eyes and its flesh was rotting. The smell was horrendous."

"I have never heard of such a thing. Are you sure?" inquired the Jarl.

"My lord Erling," said the elder lawspeaker Alvis. "Your captain's description fits how I've heard of the Draug being described by the elders of my day. It also fits with the young thrall's telling of a cat coming to him in the night trying to kill him. It is said they can shape shift into such things."

The Jarl thought on this for a few minutes before speaking again.

"Were your men able to slay the creature? This 'Draug' or dead walker thing."

"My lord," continued Hakon telling his story. "The beast was too powerful. It was on us like the speed of lightning and as powerful as we've heard in the legends of trolls. We were unable to inflict any damage upon it and were lucky to escape it."

"You weren't able to harm it in any way?" asked Jarl Erling. "There must be a way to slay this abomination."

Rowan looked up at the Jarl as if he wanted to say something, but remained quiet. Jarl Erling noticed his hesitation and spoke directly to him, "speak thrall, you may speak freely."

"My lord, I think the weapons burned it when

they hit it." Rowan explained.

The lawspeaker then said, "legend states how most unseen creatures can be harmed only with weapons made of iron. Perhaps the iron weapons burned it. It may be the key to destroying the draug."

"Yes, I have to agree." Hakon pointed out. "One of the bowmen hit the beast with arrows that had sharp iron tips. When the iron embedded in the creature, it appeared to hurt it."

"Yes my lord," Rowan recollected. "I remember when I put my master Bjord's ax into the creature's back, it appeared to have burned the creature and it struggled violently to get it out of its back. That was when I seized the moment the first time I escaped it. When it was struggling with the ax burning in its back."

There was hushed muttering by the men in the hall, all agreeing that the iron had most likely been the only thing to have hurt the creature.

Jarl Erling stood up and addressed the Hall. "Men, our village is plagued by a creature with the blood of many men on its hands. We must resolve to find a way to destroy this thing and rid ourselves of its curse before more from this village die."

Gwenda and her mother Helga arrived at the

138

Hall's door and entered just as the Jarl had made this statement.

Speaking across the Hall, she asked, "My lord, what has been discovered about the fate of my son and husband?"

She knew in her heart that Rowan's story was true. She had witnessed the hellish cat chasing the livestock. But in her heart, she had hoped that they would find her husband and son merely lost or injured and thus return them to her.

"Please, come sit." said the Jarl as he motioned for his henchmen to fetch both the blacksmith's widow and her mother a chair.

Gwenda and Helga made their way to the seats provided by the Jarl's men and quietly sat down. She kept her gaze upon the Jarl, waiting for him to deliver the news she knew he had but did not want to hear.

"Madam," said the Jarl, "Dear widow of the blacksmith, I have dire news. We have confirmed the thrall's story to have been the truth. You husband and son are dead. I am sorry."

Gwenda sank in her chair and began to weep. Helga tried to comfort her. They had already been mentally prepared to hear the bad news, but no amount of preparation can ready anyone to actually hear it being said. She has lost her husband and has also lost her only son. All the men of the household have perished. What was to become of them.

She still had the thrall, but he was unfortunately not trained in the art of blacksmithing. This was their livelihood for generations. This was a disaster to her family.

Jarl Erling tried to offer her comfort by saying, "Rest assured Madam, we will destroy the creature that killed your husband and son."

"Thank you my lord," said Gwenda. "But that won't replace him or our livelihood. Our thrall is now the only male of the household and he is not trained as a blacksmith."

Overhearing her say this, Oleg, the karl that had discovered Rowan when he originally returned, said, "I am truly sorry for the lost of your husband and of your son, but I have made a claim for finding the thrall when he was wandering outside of the village without a master."

She was flabbergasted. She couldn't believe after all that has happened, that this man had the gall to make such a claim against her household and at a time like this.

Angrily she stood up facing the man. "How dare you make a claim of property upon the death of my husband and against my household!"

"I mean no disrespect," claimed Oleg. "With the men of the household gone, the thrall is now without a legal owner and he is not a freed man. Ownership was available to whoever first claims him."

Gwenda defiantly pointed out, "my husband's property belongs to his household which passes to me now by marital right!"

The argument between them began to heat up until Jarl Erling had to silence them and call for the lawspeaker to make a legal decision on the matter.

"Lawspeaker, please recite the law of our people on this matter so we may put this dispute to rest." requested Jarl Erling.

Alvis the lawspeaker stood up and said, "It has been the custom of our people for many generations before I walked this Earth that when the father dies, the father's property fell upon to that of the first born son. If the first born was already dead, then it went to the next born son and so forth."

Oleg then pointed out, "The blacksmith Bjord's only son had been killed, leaving no other heirs or sons to claim the property because a wife does not inherit her husband's property.

Bjord's brother, Thorn spoke up and said, "Then

the property would pass to the man's family. This would make the thrall and the remaining property owned by Bjord now my property because I was his brother and his only remaining male blood kin."

The lawspeaker corrected them by saying, "This is true. However, when a son passes who has not yet become a man by his own right, then he is a man child and a child's property goes to the mother. So the thrall and the blacksmith's other properties that had passed to his son the moment Bjord died will go to the mother."

"How can that be so, when they both died?" protested Thorn.

"This is because the moment when Bjord died, his son still lived. At that point, all of what was Bjord's became that of Sven's. Then when Sven died, all that was Svens went to his mother, Gwenda." clarified Alvis.

"That is nonsense!" objected Thorn.

"In accordance to the law as has been recited by the lawspeaker," Jarl Erling declared. "All that was Bjord's had became Svens and all that was Sven's became the property of his mother Gwenda. The thrall and all of Bjord's that is now Sven's is now the property of Gwenda. This is the law, there will be no further arguments on it."

142

Oleg sat down hard upon a bench in disappointment, but accepted the ruling. He had no choice. To go against the law as recited by the lawspeaker and decreed by the Jarl would make him a criminal.

Thorn, hoping to gain a thrall and his brother bjord's properties stormed out of the hall without any further word.

'Woman, take claim of your thrall." said Jarl Erling as he pointed to Rowan, whom had been standing there confused as to what all just took place.

"Thank you, my lord."

Gwenda, assisting her mother, left the Hall with Rowan gratefully following behind them.

Rowan wasn't sure of what all had just taken place. Everything seemed to have gone by so very quickly in extremes. Nevertheless, he was glad to be out of the Jarl's Hall. He was no longer being accused of murder and no longer facing an almost certain horrible death by execution.

Chapter 11 - A Plan

Rowan laid in his bedding, which was essentially nothing more than a sack made from scrap cloth stuffed with straw and an old worn deer hide laid over it. But all things considered, it was more comfortable than sleeping on a bench or on the ground.

He laid there lost in thought as he stared out the open door into the curtain of darkness outside. It was a humid sticky night and they'd left the door open to let the cooler breeze of the night air come in.

It was relaxing to hear the nocturnal creatures at night go about their nightly routines with the smell of the fresh night breeze cleansing the stale air inside the building.

His thoughts raced through the events that had passed over the past few days. Quite a bit had happened. Life changing events that had forever changed how things would be from now on. Not only was the household of which he belonged permanently changed with a now uncertain future, but the line that divided what was real and what was fantasy was also now blurred and obscured.

As Rowan stared outside he noticed a small pair of eyes looking back at him from just outside the door in the darkness.

He was instantly alarmed by it and hastily sat up. Rowan was afraid that perhaps the dead walker had returned in some other form. Like it did when it showed up shape shifted as a cat. It could perhaps be some other creature with ill intent as well. He had no way of really knowing. He only knew that now he trusted nothing.

Rowan reached for his ax while still peering outside at the eyes cloaked in the darkness. The reflection in the eyes did not seem to be those of a critter, although by their size and proximity to the ground, it had to be a small creature.

Armed with his ax, Rowan got out of his bed and gingerly approached the door. He didn't want to wake anyone else up in the house, in case it was just a woodland creature or some other harmless critter looking to nip some food.

As he got closer to it, there was a degree of familiarity about it. Yes, the eyes in the darkness

146

were familiar to him. Indeed the eyes were not those of a hare, lynx, or even a fox.

As soon as he stepped outside the door, he heard it say, "come over here."

It was Tom Tay, that unusual creature that was in the hallow with him.

He was unsure about this Tom character, but he did save him from being discovered by the troll and Tom did lead him in the right direction to get back to his village.

Tom noticed Rowan's hesitation as he stood in the doorway pondering where to go out there or not.

"It's okay, come on out. I don't want to disturb anyone in the house. We need to talk."

At this point, curiosity was what pushed Rowan out the door. He walked outside and could see the outline of Tom hiding in the shadows. Tom looked like a very, very small man. No taller than a house cat or hare. This was very strange and made Rowan extremely nervous. He'd never seen a man so small. What kind a queer folk was Tom, he pondered.

"Why do you hide yourself?" asked Rowan.

"I don't think you're ready to gaze upon me," replied Tom. "The sight of me may frighten you and that is not my intent."

"I don't think I would be frightened," said Rowan bravely. "Especially after the things I've seen recently." he pointed out.

"Ah yes, your problem with the drauger. That is why I have called upon you this very night." said Tom. "and it's not just your problem, but a problem to your whole village."

Rowan thought about this for a moment and nodded in agreement.

'But it's not just you and your village's problem, it's a problem with all the creatures and beings in the forest as well." Tom added.

"What do you mean?" Rowan asked,

"This thing is a horrible creature that causes havoc and death to not only your people but to other things that are nature in the forest. It is an unnatural abomination that needs to be put to rest and I think you are just the person to do it."

"Oh no," said Rowan "I barely escaped with my life on both accounts of dealing with it. Both times I survived my encounters with it were nothing short of pure luck, I might add."

"Yes, but that is only because you went about it all wrong. There is something you don't know about it. That creature, like many unseen beings, has a

148

great weakness to it."

"What do you mean, are you like the dead walker?

"No, not even close. But there is something about it that we do share in common and that is a great weakness to iron."

"Iron? Why iron?" inquired Rowan.

"It's a very long story as to why, but do know that iron burns us. We can't stand it. It has something to with its unnaturalness. It is why I never enter the longhouse of your master. He is a blacksmith and there are bits of iron from his trade everywhere. Even the scent of it is foul to me and my kind. It is foul to me now as I speak to you near it."

"But the dead walker entered this longhouse, when it tried to kill me and then ran off the sheep." Rowan pointed out.

"Yes, that was very unusual. It must have been very determined to enter. At first I thought it might be as immune to iron as mankind is, but then I seen that it was hurt by iron. When you stuck the ax into it. It wasn't the ax blow that hurt it, but the fact that there was iron embedded in its flesh. The ax's iron head burned it as did the arrows that had iron tips on them."

"I did notice that, but I wasn't sure what caused it. The iron seemed to burn it as if it was red hot from the forge."

"Yes and that is how you will be able to defeat it."

"Defeat it? Like I mentioned, I barely escaped with my life ...twice. There is no way I intend to face it again. That beast killed trained warriors, some of the Jarl's best men and they were armed with iron weapons as well."

"You are right, you won't be able to defeat it directly in combat. It is too strong." Tom said.

Rowan interrupted him by reiterating, "I have no plans on battling or defeating it. My plan is to never go into the cursed forest ever again. I plan to avoid it the best as I can."

"You don't have a choice, Rowan. That creature has its mindset on you and everyone in this village. It won't stop until it kills each and everyone of you. Especially you. It seeks vengeance on you. You have to put an end to it, before it ends you."

"Why, what did I do to it?" Rowan gasped, "I'm just a thrall."

"You are not just a mere thrall, Rowan of Juteland, Son of Ingvald." said Tom.

Rowan had never heard his name in such a title

150

before. He was always, 'Rowan the thrall' or simply, the thrall.

"You have a destiny that you do not even know of yet. You do not know who you are or where you come from. You were not just a discovered orphan that was placed into servitude as a thrall. You were made as a thrall to hide you and your identity until the time had come for you to know who you are." Tom explained.

Rowan laughed at this notion and then said, "Now that I hear the name Ingvald, I do remember that my father's name was Ingvald. But I do not believe that I am anybody of any significance. I have always been just a thrall."

"Do you remember that you are not even from this land, but of another land across the sea instead. A land called Juteland." Tom asked.

"I do know that I am not from here, but I do not know where it was that I had came from."

"You came here by sea, yes?"

Rowan nodded.

"You were transported in a merchant's Knarr by a trader that had found you. But the trader who brought you and sold you to the blacksmith was no ordinary trader. He was in disguise." explained Tom.

"What do you mean?" Questioned Rowan in disbelief.

"He was to bring you to a safe place that was far away from the warring tribes that were in your homeland of Juteland. Those tribes sought to end your bloodline and slay you. He could not hide you himself, because he would have been eventually discovered. So what better way would there have been to hide you than to bring you North, disguised as a thrall."

"I have never heard such a thing. I think you may be mistaken." said Rowan.

"By not letting you know who you really were was the best way to keep your true identity a secret. Not even the blacksmith knew. When he purchased you to be his thrall, he swore an oath to sell you back for double the price without any question when the trader came back for you years later. He also swore an oath to tell no one of this promise that he made to the trader."

Rowan stood quietly for a moment taking all this in. He remembered one night when the blacksmith was drunk from taking in too much mead and told Rowan that he was only temporarily his thrall. He had no idea what Bjord meant by that, nor ever asked. He just assumed it as being drunk talk. Nevertheless the statement had stuck with him.

"So who am I and what is this alleged destiny?" asked Rowan.

"That is not important right now. What is important is...."

"What do you mean it is not important right now? " Rowan asked as he interrupted Tom. "Then why did you tell me such a thing?"

"It is not important right now, because it is not your time yet. You time will come and then everything will be explained to you." Answered Tom. "But it is not your time to die and the only way to stop your death is if you slay the creature before it comes for you."

"How do you know its even coming for me?" asked Rowan.

"Because it has been my task to watch over you and I have seen the creature come to the edge of the woods near here and look upon this very house. It has been seeking you. It is only a matter of time until it comes for you. It came for you before and was unsuccessful killing you in your sleep. But only because it was weakened by the iron in the house. It won't fail again. Especially now that it is angry." stressed Tom.

"If it wanted to kill me, why didn't it kill me both times when I was near its lair?"

"It's a creature that has been risen from the abyss of death. It is not very smart and it was distracted. That's the only reason it did not come after you blindly. Had it been, it would have destroyed you easily."

"I have no doubt of that. It is too powerful. I don't think it's even possible for me to kill it as you seem to think I am able to do." expressed Rowan.

"I have a plan that might work." explained Tom. "The iron not only hurts the creature, but also weakens it. You can use the creature's weakness against it."

"How so?" asked Rowan.

"I think you can use the scraps of iron within this longhouse and make a trap."

Rowan laughed and asked, "how would I possibly make a trap with scraps of iron?"

"You must use your imagination and think!"

Rowan could sense the annoyance in Tom's voice.

"Okay, but you said you had a plan. You must understand, I have never trapped a huge monster before. Or anything else for that matter." pointed out Rowan. "You said you had a plan. What is your plan?"

"Find a net and string bits of iron all through it.

Make a trap and lure the monster into it. When the net with iron falls upon it, it will be trapped and unable to get the iron netting off before you can attack it. We believe that you can kill it if you chop it's head off and burn it." explained Tom.

"Wait a minute, who's 'we.'" inquired Rowan, not missing Tom's accidental use of 'we' instead of 'I.'

"Again, that is not important right now. When the time is right, I promise you, all your questions will be answered." Tom insisted.

"But how am I to do all of this anyways? The lady of the house, my mistress Gwenda, will never allow me to leave nor will she allow me to take any iron. She plans to sell it all to traders." Rowan explained. "They plan to trade wool and other items tomorrow. I am suppose to take care of the livestock and gather iron fror her while they're away. There is no way I'll have time."

"Don't worry about any of that. I will come in tomorrow after you leave and take care of everything in the household." Tim promised. "You focus on the task at hand."

Chapter 12 - The Trap

The very next morning after the women of the house had left for the day, Rowan began getting ready. It would be his only window of opportunity as the ladies of the house had planned to spend the entire day in the village center to trade. Many knarrs with traders were expected to show up and Gwenda had hopes that she'd be able to trade wool and other goods.

Nobody else would be in the longhouse today, so Rowan took his chance to set his plan into action. Gwenda had tasked him to take care of the livestock and clean up her late husband's blacksmithing items to be traded later.

Tom had promised Rowan that he'd take care of everything that needed to be done when Rowan was absent. Excluding the iron blacksmith items, of course.

Tom said he'd show up after Rowan left to deal

with the draug. Rowan had no choice but to hope
Tom kept his word and showed up after he left. For
now, he had to get busy if he had any hope of
completing this dreadful task that laid ahead.

Rowan gathered up as much iron items as he
could. Iron scraps, pieces of slag, pig iron, whatever
he could find. There were two unfinished shirts of
chain mail that Bjord had been working on. Rowan
grabbed those as well. He figured that he could use
them to help trap the beast.

It was a heavy load and he was already
struggling with it. He had two wooden buckets full
of assorted scrap iron, a sling with 15 ax heads
strung on it, and two partial shirts of chain mail. He
also grabbed the fisherman's net that Bjord had
hanging in the rafters, along with some assorted
twine and rope. He had quite a load to carry.

He decided to divide the weight on a yoke they
had for carrying the milk. It was a shoulder pole
which he could put over his shoulder to help bear
the weight through the forest and up the hillside.

Rowan tied as much as he could to the shoulder
pole, including Bjord's ax, and put the heavy load on
his shoulder. It was heavy, but not as bad as he
thought it would be.

Taking one last look behind him at the longhouse,

he made his was through the forest and up the hill towards the draug's burial mound.

Rowan's mind drifted here and there as he made the walk. This was his third time taking this path and he no longer needed to track it. He unfortunately knew the way by heart by now.

There were some serious doubts in his thinking as to whether or not he'd be successful doing this. He tried to think of ways to make his trap plan work out, but most of his thoughts wandered on the fact that he felt this was his last trip to the creature's mound.

Not because he felt he would successfully trap and kill it, but because he felt his best efforts would be futile and the draug was certain to kill him.

By time he made it to the area just before where the dead walker's mound was located, he was already covered in sweat from bearing the load and keeping a steady pace with only short rests. He only stopped to rest long enough to catch his breath. He wanted to get up to the location while he still had plenty of daylight to work in.

Looking around at the pathway through the bushes, he could smell the creature's foul scent of death and knew it was close. He tried to be quiet and not attract its attention, even though he assumed it didn't matter as the creature could probably sense him anyways.

Most of all, he tried not to look at the bodies of the brave men who had taken him up there to prove his story about the creature in the first place. Their bodies laid where they had fallen when they tried to fight the beast. Seeing their mangled corpses didn't help Rowan's confidence in that he'd be able to do this by himself one bit.

This was a place of death begat by death.

Trying to keep focused, Rowan set down his load and set to work as quickly as he could. He had to quickly make the trap if he'd any hope of successfully pulling it off. That is, if his plan would work at all or if the iron would even stop the accursed beast.

Casting these negative thoughts to the wind, Rowan began to make the snare. Initially, he was going to dig a pit and make a dead fall for the creature, but in his haste to gather iron he'd forgotten to bring a shovel.

He could use his the ax and his hands, but it would still take too much time to prepare and the creature would probably show up before he got the hole dug anyways.

Thinking better, he decided to make a snare to

trip the creature or at least slow it down enough so he could get the net over it ...somehow.

Rowans laid out the fishing net. It wasn't as big as he wanted it to be, but it would do. He used the twine he brought to tie in bits of iron sporadically in the net. The idea was when the net was over the creature, the iron would be pressing on it at multiple locations.

He took the rope he had and cut several lengths. With the rope lengths he made a knot about a forearm's length apart from each other. In between each knot, he threaded an ax head through the rope length.

In his plan, once he got the net over the creature, hopefully slowing it down, he could wrap the rope around in and bind the beast with the iron ax heads pressed against it and further disable it.

He hung the net from some limbs above and tied knots holding the net to limbs that he could pull loose with a single length of rope. He tied the net up a couple times and pulled the rope loose to make sure it would work as planned. Also so he'd know exactly where it would drop.

At the spot where the net dropped, he laid the chain mail shirts down and tied them together so they were wide. He threaded rope around the blanket of chain mail and tossed the rope over a strong limb above.

He bent a young tree down and tied it down to the ground. Then he tied the rope leading to the chain mail to the bent over tree.

Now all he had to do was cut the rope holding the tree bent over and it spring back up and pull the chain mail up tight around the beast's legs. He concealed the chain mail with leaves, so the draug wouldn't see it. Also so the iron wouldn't burn its feet right away, exposing the trap.

He set his ax down by the tied off rope, so it would be ready. If everything went to plan, all he had to do was lure the creature into the spot, pull the rope so the net dropped on it and then cut the rope holding the tree down so it would pull the chain mail up over its legs. After the net was dropped on it and the chainmail sprung up on it, all he had to do was grab the rope with the iron ax heads threaded through it and wrap the rope around the beast while it was snared.

The rest of his plan relied on using Bjord's ax to finish the creature off.

Plan B entailed running away as fast as he could. In truth, there was no plan B. This had to work.

Chapter 13 - The Battle

A couple hours had passed since Rowan had finished making the trap. He'd been sitting on the ground holding the rope to the net and watching the passageway to the dead walker's burial mound. Watching and waiting for it to come.

He hoped that he could safely wait there and the draug would just come from, well wherever it came from by the mound, and just head towards him so he could trap it. But that obviously wasn't going to happen. He was going to have to expose himself and lure the creature to his trap.

Rowan didn't like this idea, because there was a great chance he'd never get the creature to the trap and an even greater chance the creature would kill him before he even had the chance to trap it.

This was why he waited in this spot, putting the trap between him and the passageway where the creature usually came from. It was the safest way.

Unfortunately, the safest way was not going to work. He had no choice but to try and lure it in.

Reluctantly, Rowan got up from the ground and grabbed the ax he'd set up to cut the snare line and started walking towards the passageway to the beast's mound.

Already he could feel his heart pounding in both anticipation and fear.

Taking slow steps, he walked through the passageway through the bush and looked at the mound. He stood there and tried to come up with a way he could lure the beast out into the open, chase him and lead it to the trap...without it killing him.

There was no real to do it safely.

"Do it safely." Rowan quietly said to himself, "What a joke. Safely isn't even a word that belonged in this predicament."

It was all or nothing time. Rowan abruptly walked to the burial mound and kicked some of the rocks loose.

Anticipating the beast to show up, literally anywhere, he held the ax at the ready and looked around in every direction.

Nothing.

This time he stood on the mound and kicked

more rocks off of it. Hoping to disturb it. He knew it was in there. He knew that was where it came out from when it formed from a strange mist.

Rowan stood on the mound for a few minutes, turning in every direction. He watched for the beast or any mist to come up. There was still nothing. This wasn't going to plan in any shape or form.

He simply wasn't going to be able to lure the beast out of its mound. A huge part of him was glad for that. Even though he'd show up and carried out the plan with a mockery of bravery that really didn't exist. It was more in desperation that led him to carry out this plan brought to him by Tom - a creature he wasn't even sure about.

There was only a few hours of daylight left and Rowan figured it would probably be best to gather the iron back up and carry it back down before his mistress Gwenda came back home.

Being that he wasn't successful in getting himself killed with this hair-brained plan, he may as well not get in trouble for taking the iron and going into the forest as well.

Rowan started walking back to fetch the items he used for his trap, but as he started walking through the passage through the bush, he noticed the tell-tale mist forming from the creature.

"Here it comes!" Rowan thought as his heart sank. He'd already been grateful that the creature didn't show, now it's here and it's go time.

Rowan slowly turned around and looked towards the mound. There it stood, the grotesques dead walker the elders called a draug.

It had formed in the mist when Rowan had his back turned. Apparently, it sought to ambush him.

Rowan looked directly at it as it looked right back at him.

This was a VERY bad idea.

Rowan immediately darted off at full speed towards his trap. If he could get to the rope before it reached the drop spot, he'd have a chance to trap it. It was the only chance he had. He knew he'd never outrun it and escape. It had to be trapped otherwise he was now trapped.

Rowan ran with everything he had. He could hear the beast howl angrily at him and its footsteps stomping behind him. It was chasing him.

He got past the passageway and was heading to the rope. He had to get to it. Rowan never ran so fast in his life. He was in sheer panic. But just as he was stepping over the chainmail hidden under the leaves, his foot caught a piece of rope and he tripped.

Rowan tumbled face first over his trap and rolled out of control on the ground, dropping his ax and everything.

He quickly recovered and looked for the ax. It was on the ground next to the chain mail snare trap. He ran to grab it and seen that the beast was charging straight for him.

As soon as Rowan picked up the ax the beast was on him. He recovered and stood back up just as the creature swung at him. It barely missed his head as it drove its monstrosity of a fist into the ground.

Rowan swung the ax and hit it in the leg, cutting it deeply. It was a panic swing, but he hit it soundly. The creature roared in anger as Rowan turned to swing his ax and cut the rope so he could snare the beast.

Unfortunately. when Rowan hit the rope with his ax it didn't cut the rope and only bounced off of it.

Thinking quickly while the creature was still in the trap spot, Rowan turned and pulled the other rope and released the fisherman's net with the iron ties on it.

The net dropped as planned, but did not land on the creature completely. Part of it fell to the side, but enough of it fell over the creature's head and shoulder, allowing the net to cover half of its body.

The iron trick was working. The beast was furiously howling in pain as the iron laid on its flesh and burned it.

It swung around madly trying to get the net off of it. Rowan noticed it was standing directly over the chain mail snare with both feet now. He tried to cut the rope with his ax again. The ax bounced off the rope once again, only cutting a few threads of the rope.

Frustrated, Rowan swung the ax and cut the rope where he had it tied down. This time it cut through and released the snare.

The tree Rowan bent down sprung back up, puling the rope and thus pulling the chain mail up and around the creature's feet.

It screeched in a furious madness as the chain mail wrapped around its legs and feet. The iron burned it wherever it touched the creature's cursed dead flesh.

Remembering the rope strung with iron, Rowan quickly grabbed it from the ground and threw it around the dead walker as it was trying to get itself lose from the netting. Rowan managed to get it around it legs and ran around the creature as it roared at him. He wrapped the roped around the beast several times and then pulled at it taut.

170

He was trying to knock the creature over but failed because it was too heavy to even budge. It was like trying to pull an oak tree down, the forsaken being was extremely heavy and stood soundly firm in its place.

Rowan ran around the other side of it to grab his ax once again and try to hack it down.

However, as Rowan picked up the ax from the ground where he'd tossed it to pick up the rope with ax heads ties in it, the creature made a move for him.

The draug tried to step towards Rowan and swing at him, but tripped over the entanglement of chain mail and iron laced rope wrapped around it.

The dead walker fell to the ground and howled as it struggled to get itself free. This was the opportunity Rowan needed. He picked up the battle ax with both hands and lifted it above his head. He took one last look at the creature before he brought the ax down on its head with all his might.

The dull thud announced the ax hitting its mark. A grotesque sight indeed as the undead thing emitted a low growl.

Surprisingly, it was still alive. Such a direct blow to the head like that would have ended any living being. Yet this thing wasn't even really alive. This cursed thing shouldn't even be walking around in the first place. It had been already dead at one time and then risen again by some unknown strange reason to reap its malice upon the world.

With difficultly, Rowan pulled the ax from the thing's head. It was too deeply embedded and he had to put his foot on the thing's chest to gain leverage as he freed the ax.

The creature, although greatly weakened from the iron, persevered in its struggle to get free.

Rowan knew what he had to do; there was only one way to end all of this madness. Gulping in disappoint to the task of which he had to preform, he raised the bloodied ax over his head once again and this time aimed for the creature's neck. He swung down with all his force and struck the draug's swollen, unnatural neck.

It took Rowan two more chops to separate the creature's head from its body. The abomination's body was so large and had swollen to such an unnatural size, there was nothing simple about it.

To Rowan's relief, once the head was detached the creature's body stopped moving and went limp.

Horrifically, even though the body appeared to be dead, the creature's head was still alive!

Rowan grabbed the head by its hair and lifted it

up to look it.

Its dead, lifeless white eyes were still open as was the mouth as well. The thing was actually trying to growl, although the only sound emitting from it was a drowned incongruous gurgling sound.

Repulsed by it, Rowan tossed the head on the ground. He rolled it over with his foot so that its face was towards the ground so he didn't have to look at it.

He knew what he had to do at this point. The burden of his dirty work was not yet complete. There was simply too much risk of this thing coming back alive. The only way to make sure it was dead and stayed dead was to burn it.

Rowan began gathering dead wood that was around the area and started stacking the firewood on top of the creature's corpse.

At first he was going to dig a hole, roll the creature in it and then burn it in the hole so it could be easily covered up. But when he tested out this plan he discovered that the beast simply was too great in weight. The thing's headless body was uncannily heavy. He wasn't able to budge it in even the slightest manner. It was like a solid rock that would take a team of horses to move.

So he decided to burn it on the ground where it

laid.

He would need proof of killing it however. Although he was not happy about having to deal with its still-alive head, he really had no choice. He would have carry it back to the Jarl as proof of the creature's demise.

Rowan gathered the ghastly still active head with its dull gurgling growl and placed it in one of the buckets he used to carry the iron scraps up the mountain.

Having gathered enough firewood to make a fire big enough to burn the creature's body to ash, Rowan set the hastily built funeral pyre on fire.

He watched the black smoke of the great fire roll into the sky for a couple hours until he was satisfied that the corpse was going to be reduced to ash, never to rise a again.

The Sun was only an hour or less until it was going to set for the day. Rowan made a torch and lit it from the bonfire's blaze. He gathered his things, including the bucket with the moaning head in it, and made his way down the mountainside towards the village.

174

Chapter 14 - The Triumphant Return

Rowan arrived at the village's edge just a few hours after night fall. He pondered for a moment trying to decide where to go. Either to the longhouse of his mistress, the blacksmith's wife and wait until morning to announce his defeating the dead walker; Or to continue on and go to the Great Hall of the Jarl now.

One thing was for certain, he needed to take a short break first. He was exhausted. Even though he killed the creature, he didn't want to be in the mountain's forest at night. The now defeated creature wasn't the only threat that laid within the forest and on the mountain. Rowan had come to learn there were many things in the wilderness that were more of a threat than wolves and bears.

He set his bundle down, thankful of the moonlight that lit the way. The moonlight enabled him to trek through the last stretch of forest. His torch had burned itself out already and he didn't make another because he was somewhat still able to see without using a torch. Even though he could have devised one rather quickly with a dried branch before the previous one burned itself out, he decided not to bother and keep going.

Feeling rested enough from taking a short 'breather,' Rowan gathered up his things and made his way towards the Great Hall. He knew the Jarl and a majority of the men of the village would the there. There simply was no better time to do this than now.

It wasn't long until Rowan was standing just outside the Great Hall. He could hear the muffled voices of the men inside. He set everything down by the outside wall and retrieved only the bucket containing the head. He could still hear its muffled groans. It was strange how this body-less head was still alive.

He walked up to the doorway and stood there a moment. He was still hesitant to just walk inside. As he was just a lowly thrall and wasn't exactly permitted to enter without a master or without a really good reason.

Silly thought. This was reason enough, he reassured himself as he gathered the courage to enter.

178

As soon as he stepped foot in the Hall, his presence was immediately noticed by men near the door. One was about to confront him, but another man standing next to him, seeing what Rowan was carrying in the bucket, stopped him.

A guard that was standing by the door who had also seen what Rowan was carrying, called out loud enough to be heard above the other conversing voices and merriment in the Hall, "My Lord!"

The hall quickly went quiet as everyone turned and looked at Rowan. The guard motioned Rowan to go to the Jarl and followed behind him as he walked towards the Jarl.

As Rowan walked toward the end of the Hall where the Jarl was seated, men stepped aside and allowed him passage. Whispers and murmurs grew among the men, as they inquired amongst each other as to what was going on and why the thrall was in the Hall.

With a degree of uneasiness Rowan walked past all the gawking men, whom at first looked upon him disparagingly until they seen what he was carrying inside of his bucket.

Rowan made his way past everyone and stood before the Jarl, whom was sitting in his throne looking at him with a questioning expression on his face. Rowan tried to keep his eyes lowered, not wanting to provoke anyone's wrath upon him, especially that of the Jarl.

As soon as he got in front of the Jarl's throne, he set the bucket down before the Jarl's feet and took a step back before he kneeling down.

"My Lord, I present to you the dead walker's head."

The Hall lit up in an almost instant roar upon hearing Rowan say this. Some voices cheering the creature's vanquish, while others contested it with their doubts.

The Jarl leaned forward in his chair and looked in the bucket. Seeing the back of the grotesque bloodied head of the creature, he was immediately revolted by the sight of it.

Even though the Jarl was a seasoned warrior who had seen many battles, he still didn't like the sight of blood or dead things. But he was the leader and he couldn't show even an ounce of weakness, no matter how much this thing repulsed him.

Needing to verify the thrall's claim, he reached down into the bucket and flipped the head over so he could see its face. As soon as he flipped the head over, he quickly pulled his hand back and stood up.

The room quietened when they seen him stand up so fast.

Jarl Erling looked at Rowan and then turned his gaze to the other men in the hall and announced, "The beast has been slain!"

The Jarl's confirmation caused the room to erupt in cheers.

He then sat back down and looked at Rowan and asked, "the head is still alive?"

Rowan nodded. "Yes my Lord, the body died when I chopped its head off, but the head somehow remained alive."

There was gasping by the men who peered over and looked at the head in the bucket. Rowan could hear the talk behind him as many of the men in the room debated whether it was the creature's head or not. There were many men trying to step forward and look over each other to see the head to verify this for themselves.

The Jarl called over to one of his guards and told him to fetch the lawspeaker. The guard nodded and immediately turned, making his way through the crowd before disappearing out the Hall's door.

Seeing how the men inside of the Hall were crowding each other, trying to see the creature's head inside of the bucket, the Jarl stood up and said, "Calm down men. There is no need to crowd each other."

The Jark reached down while being careful not to let the thing bite him and pulled the head up out of the bucket. Unfortunately, as soon as he picked it up, it slipped from his grip and fell back into the bucket making a barely audible thud sound when it landed.

The nasty rotting thing repulsed him, but again he kept it hidden from his men. Rowan, however, was able to see the Jarl's distaste at touching it and offered to take it out of the bucket.

"My Lord, there is no need for you to touch such a repulsive and vile thing. Please allow me."

The Jarl nodded. "Place it on the floor so all may see it."

Rowan nodded and carefully reached into the bucket and picked up the creature's head. He held onto its ears so it wouldn't slip out of his hands as it did when the Jarl tried to pick it up. Rowan lifted the head up and turned to face the men in the hall. He held the head up high above his head for a moment so everyone in the Hall could get a good look at it before setting the head down on the ground.

Rowan made sure the head was upright and facing the hall, so everyone could examine it as they pleased. He then wiped his hands on his tunic and stepped back, away from the head on the ground. Rowan knelt to the side so he would still be facing the Jarl, but also so he could see the head and the men in the hall.

Rowan was permitted to quietly just kneel there and began getting barraged by questions from the men in the Hall about how he managed to kill the dead walker and why was the head still alive.

The Jarl interrupted their inquiries and announced, "be patient until the lawspeaker arrives and everyone shall have their questions answered. Leave the thrall be for the moment."

The creature's head was still looking around with its dead eyes and occasionally emitted a growl. Although the muffled growls could barely be heard now over the noise in the Hall. Everyone looking at it could still see its mouth move as it was trying to growl and roar.

Another man pushed his way through to get a glimpse of the dead walker's head and angrily asked, "How did you possibly kill it. There is no way a mere thrall could have done such a thing. Especially after it slayed so many seasoned warriors."

As Rowan was about to answer the man's question, Jarl Erling calmly lifted his hand signaling

Rowan to not answer.

"I sent for the Lawspeaker. We shall wait to hear what happened when the Lawspeaker arrives and only then. I want him to hear the details as well so we can get his take on all of this."

Seeing how many of the men were growing impatient, the Jarl said in a louder voice, "Please men, just be patient and enjoy the mead I have provided. Your wait for answers and to hear the thrall's story should not be very much longer. I sent for Alvis the Lawspeaker. He should be here any moment."

The Jarl had his own thralls bring more mead to be distributed in the Hall. Many of the men settled down and took in the mead, compliments of the Jarl's hospitality.

The wait for the Lawspeaker wasn't much longer as he finally arrived, assisted by the Housekarl that was sent to fetch him. The elderly man was seated in a chair provided for him in front of the Jarl, so he could see the head on the floor.

The old wise man examined the gruesome head for a few minutes from his chair without saying a word as the Jarl and everyone else looked on. The men in the Hall were discussing it among themselves and coming up with their own conclusions. After a

184

few moments, the old man stopped looking at it and relaxed in his chair. He looked up at the Jarl and nodded, indicating that he ready to speak.

The Jarl stood up and raised his hands up and said, "Quiet! Men, I need the Hall to quieten."

The Hall began to quieten with the help of a few men telling the other men, relaying the Jarl's command.

When the Hall fell silent and with everyone's attention, Jarl Erling announced, "Now Alvis the wise, bearer of our laws, is ready to hear the thrall Rowan's testimony. The thrall named Rowan will now speak."

The Jarl sat down and motioned the now wide eyed Rowan to speak.

"Tell us Rowan, how you've come to possess the head of the very creature that has slayed our men and become a plague to this village."

Feeling ever uncertain, especially because the last time he was forced to speak before the Hall he was accused and was nearly executed for murder, Rowan obediently stood up and began to tell his story.

"The first two times that we confronted the creature, it was noticed that iron hurt it. In fact, it appeared to have burned it. I knew something had to be done about this creature because I knew it wasn't going to leave the folk of this village alone."

"What makes you think that?" blurted out a man. "Perhaps if we left it be, it would leave us be."

A few other men in the Hall agreed with him.

"Because we didn't even know it existed until it came to kill one of us in the night. It preying upon some of our livestock permitted us to track it to its lair." Rowan stressed. "Whatever drove this creature, wasn't going to stop. It came after us and you can bet it was going to come back, again and again."

"Okay let's say that it was going to keep coming back. What was your idea?" asked one man.

"I noticed the iron hurt the creature, so I thought I would be able to use iron to trap and kill it."

Many men listening were nodding in agreement to Rowan's rationalization.

"So I gathered up a net, some rope, and lots of scrap iron. I made a trap to lure the creature into. I figured if I found a way to cover the beast in iron, it would weaken and I'd have the opportunity to slay it.

"Did this work?"

"Yes." Rowan motioned towards the beast's head on the floor. "I was able to lure it into a trap and get the iron wrapped around it. Once it was subdued, I tried to kill it.

"Tried to kill it? Didn't it die easily once it was subdued with the iron?"

"No, as you can see on its head. I tried to bury my ax in its head but it did not kill the creature. So I chopped its head off instead. It was then that its body died, when Its head was severed off. But strangely, its head remained alive. Even now, the head lives without its body."

"Where is the dead walker's body now?"

"I stacked wood over its body in a sort of funeral pyre and burnt it. It was the only way I could be sure it would not come back to life."

"What made you think it would come back to life and needed to be burned?"

"Because the head was still alive, I didn't want to chance the body coming back alive."

"It was a wise move." Jarl Erling said. "To burn the body. That way there would be no way the creature could come back or its body searching for its head."

After hearing Rowan's story, the men in the hall began debating among themselves and exchanging their own personal feelings on the matter. Some were deciding whether or not they believed Rowan's story.

The head Rowan brought back was undeniable proof that he'd accomplished killing the creature. The fact that the head was still alive was also proof it was indeed the creature. It was undeniably something unnatural.

After a few moments of discussion, the Jarl finally stood up and said, "Quiet men, we have heard the thrall's account and he indeed has brought proof of the creature's death....well, mostly dead, as the head remains alive. We must now hear what the lawspeaker has to say after hearing all of this."

Jarl Erling turned towards the Alvis the lawspeaker and said, "Tell us wise one, what do you know of such things. Would he have been able to end this creature and why is the head still alive. Tell us what black magic this is that keeps the abomination's head alive?"

The lawspeaker spoke as loud as his frail elderly voice would allow.

"I have not seen a dead walker personally, but I do remember an incident with one when I was a young boy. Our village was under attack much like this one was and men had been dispatched to kill it. After a several failed attempts and the loss of lives to several brave men, they did finally manage to kill it.

188

It was said that they burned the remains of the monster. They had rid it permanently by burning it. I do not know why this creature's head is still alive, that is something of knowledge that perhaps the Völva would be able to tell us. The creature that plagued us, they never separated the head and burned all of it when they finally managed to slay it"

The Jarl nodded, acknowledging what the Lawspeaker was saying. "We will have to send for the Völva from the neighboring village and see what knowledge she has of this creature, if any."

The old man nodded his head agreeing with the Jarl and said, "She may or may not know why, but she may know of some lore as to why we were plagued by this creature in the first place. Perhaps something we should have done straight away to rid ourselves of it or prevent another one like it from coming in the future."

The Jarl raised his eyebrows and nodded his head. "I agree."

The old man then turned to Rowan and said, "It was a good thing you didn't just bury it. The creature probably would have risen again, with or without its head."

There seemed to be much agreement in the Hall with the wise lawspeaker's statement.

"Did you know there was a reward for killing it?" The Jarl asked Rowan.

"No, my lord. I am not aware of any reward for killing the creature." Answered Rowan, shaking his head.

It was true, Rowan wasn't aware of any kind award. This was new information to him and was also somewhat puzzling to him. He wasn't sure what was to happen now. He instantly grew worried, because the last time he'd come into this Hall he'd been accused of murder and almost lost his life. He remembered how he was chained to a pole as well. He wore a neck ring, but it was always just symbolic of his status as a thrall. The blacksmith never chained him to anything, not even once.

As these thoughts of uncertainty raced around in his mind, the Jarl called out to one of his guards.

"Someone fetch Gwenda Helgasdottir, the blacksmith's widow. She is the one that owns this thrall. She needs to be here. Get her at once!"

One of the guards in the back of the Hall called out, "I shall get her, my Lord" and swiftly exited out the door.

It wasn't very long until Gwenda arrived with the guard. Although the wait seemed even longer to Rowan as his mind ran through different scenarios as to what his fate was going to be. He was now regretting ever going off into the forest and slaying the creature at this point.

As Gwenda walked through the Hall to the Jarl's throne, the men in Hall hushed as they pondered what was to happen next. Rowan wasn't the only one curious as to what was going to happen next.

The Jarl called for a chair to be brought for her and was met with immediate compliance by one of the guards that set down a chair on the other side of Rowan, opposite of the old lawspeaker. When she got to where they were seated, she noticed the head on the floor and immediately cowered from it, openly repulsed.

"My pardons lady for not having that put up before you entered." the Jarl said apologetically.

Without needing the Jarl's instruction to do so, Rowan stepped up and put the head back in the bucket. A guard appeared with a cloth and used it to cover the bucket so she wouldn't be forced to look upon it.

She thanked the guard and the Jarl for their consideration. Secretly, the Jarl was glad for her arrival and for having an excuse to cover the repulsive thing.

"That head belongs to the beast that is

responsible for slaying your son and husband." Jarl Erling explained.

"Thank you, my lord, for reaping vengeance on behalf of my family." she replied.

Standing up and facing the men within the Hall, she graciously announced to them all.

"My greatest gratitude to the Hero of our Folk who has slayed this beast and rid our people of any further harm from it."

She looked around the Hall to see who would come forward to state they were the one that slayed the creature, but nobody did.

"Please hero, show yourself. My family owes you the greatest of our gratitude." she plead.

Jarl Erling stood up and approached Gwenda and put his hands on her shoulders. "My fair lady, your hero is your very own thrall." he said as he pointed to Rowan, whom was still knelling and looking down upon the ground, not sure what to do or say.

She was taken back upon hearing this and replied with a surprised, "my thrall?"

"Lady, did you send your thrall out to slay the creature?"

"No, my lord. I didn't even know he had left to

192

do such a thing." she replied. "We were out trading all day and I wasn't even aware our thrall was missing until we came home to find him missing."

At this point, Rowan's heart sank. Just what he needed, to be accused of trying to escape again. That was a punishable offense. Even by death if his master or mistress so desired.

Jarl Erling stood up and addressed the hall.

"The thrall named Rowan, without permission from his mistress nor with the intent of collecting the bounty for slaying the dead walker that was plaguing our village, took it upon himself to go out alone and kill the wretched thing with no plan for compensation or reward. He did this for the better of the people of this village and has achieved alone what none of our best men could achieve. This is a selfless and heroic act that must be recognized!"

There were cheers of approval within the Hall. This announcement startled Rowan, who just a moment ago was expecting the worse and was even starting to regret killing the beast.

Jarl Erling stepped in front of Rowan and commanded, "Rise Thrall!"

Rowan nervously rose to his feet, still unsure as to what was about to happen.

"The bounty I made for the slaying of the beast was 500 silver pieces. Because of this thrall's selfless act of bravery, he is no longer worthy of being that of a mere thrall. That would be a disgrace. With the bounty, I pay his mistress the weregeld value of a useful thrall of 60 silver pieces."

A guard was standing next to the Jarl at this point holding a fine leather bag, obviously full of silver pieces.

Jarl Erling counted out 60 pieces of silver from it and handed it to Gwenda, whom sat there bewildered with an uncertain look on her face. She was relieved to have the deaths of her son and husband revenged, but she didn't expect to lose her thrall. This was a problem, but she knew she could not speak up against the Jarl's decision.

"Having paid for ownership of the thrall as property of my own, I announce before everyone that he is no longer a thrall, but a freeman." Jarl Erling announced to the hall.

There was much talk in the Hall as voices grew louder. Some cheering Rowan and the Jarl, others protesting because they didn't like the thrall being freed.

"Not only do I make him a new freeman, I make him a Karl. Because he is to be regarded as a hero, braver than any man I have seen in my realm as of yet. He will not have the short status of a newly free'd thrall who is only above a thrall in status, but still below freemen and karls until three generations of freedmen descended from him as is customary with our folk. He is to have the status of Karl and be regarded as a hero."

"He's not a Karl," grumbled one man.

"He's a mere thrall and is being freed and given a status higher than the rest of the men of this village. How is that fair to our folk?" grumbled another man.

This last statement caused some uproar in the Hall. Jarl Erling immediately put an end to it.

"I have seen not one man do what this man has done. He has earned the status and the right and no man will argue it, lest he disgrace himself and the people of this realm." Jarl Erling then pointed at Rowan. "Have his neck ring removed at once, he is no longer a thrall! We will celebrate his honor!"

Rowan stood there, still in shock of what had just happened. Jarl Erling handed Rowan the sack of silver and placed it in his hand.

"The remaining reward bounty is yours."

Rowan took hold of the small bag of silver, stunned as he'd never had money before. The Jarl turned and returned to his throne. A few men stepped forward and patted Rowan on the back, congratulating him. It was a strange feeling to Rowan. He had never been treated as an equal or even acknowledged him as a human being. Now they were treating him as one of their own.

One man came in with tools and removed the pin from Rowan's neck ring. He pulled the neck ring off and handed it to Gwenda whom was still sitting her chair flabbergasted. She took the neck ring and quietly left.

Rowan, still looking down at the bag of silver and feeling unusually 'naked' due to no longer wearing his neck ring, was handed a drinking horn personally by the Jarl.

He looked up and accepted the Jarl's offer of mead. The Jarl satisfied, turned towards the rest of the men in the Hall and said, "drink up everyone and feast at my table."

He turned back towards Rowan and pointed at the main table in the Hall which had various meats.

"Eat and be merry as my guest, Hero Rowan. Tomorrow, you will swear your allegiance to me and receive your arm ring."

Rowan looked around the Hall at his strange new World through the eyes of a freeman. Things were

196

different now. He was going to have to learn how to
live as a Karl and make a life for himself.

But tonight, he was drinking from the Jarl's cup.
A thrall brought Rowan and chunk of meat and
some bread. The meat was one of the best cuts,
something Rowan never had before. He savored it.

Up on the rafters above in a dark corner,
unnoticed by anyone in Hall, quietly sat the wee
Tom Tay. Quite pleased with himself, as he watched
as his plan played itself out successfully.

There was still much to do. But the time was
finally coming. Tom would make sure Rowan took
the right path to fulfill his destiny. And every now
and then, make things happen to speed things along
smoothly.

** The End of the Beginning**